Praise for INVADER

"Fans of sci-fi mysteries and strong female characters should snap up this psychological page-turner." —*Publishers Weekly*

"A cunningly plotted novel that keeps readers guessing with twists and turns and an ending they won't see coming."
—The Booklife Prize

"A gritty, tense psychological thriller. A RED RIBBON WINNER and highly recommended."
—The Wishing Shelf Book Awards

"A short, briskly paced novel that's full of entertaining plot twists." —*Kirkus Reviews*

"Highly recommended for readers who enjoy surprising twists of plot, mysteries, and stories that quickly move into delightfully unexpected realms of psychological recovery…"
—*Midwest Book Review*

"What a compelling read. The tension immediately established in the first chapter works well to captivate the reader, holding one's attention until the big reveal."
—Judge, 27th Annual Writer's Digest S-P Book Awards

"This is one of the best books ˥ ˙˙˙˙ᵈ in the last few years, and I can't recom
—Author & blogger Boris ˢ

D1052592

INVADER

MARJORY KAPTANOGLU

The Book Reality Experience

For my sisters and brothers:

Kay Liscomb
Mine Günceler
Jim Benedict
Sabo Günceler
Bill Liscomb

Siblings are the people we practice on,
the people who teach us about fairness and
cooperation and kindness and caring —
quite often the hard way.

-Pamela Dugdale

Chapter One

ROSE

HER FIRST SENSATION was of a man's arms around her, lifting her out of the sea. He carried her over the sand to a dry patch of ground, where he laid her down. She turned her face, coughed, and spat out saltwater.

"You all right?" the man said.

She squinted up at him, unable to make out his features with the stark sun blazing behind his head. A feeling of foreboding gripped her and caused a shiver.

"Let me help you," he said. The man raised her into a sitting position.

She stared at her arm, wondering why it felt like she'd never seen her own hand before. Her gaze shifted to her legs, which seemed like they belonged to some other person. She felt her eyes, nose and lips, trying to remember what her face looked like. She squeezed the dampness from her long reddish hair, waiting for her memory to return.

When it didn't, she looked up, taking in the stunning blue of the cloudless sky, the glittering sand, and the jungle trees bordering the beach, continuing high into the distant hills. The beauty of her surroundings soothed her. The breeze brushed her face and she closed her eyes while she drew in a deep breath. The air smelled salty and briny and yet that also brought pleasure.

Items scattered along the shore caught her attention. Some rope, a piece of torn sail, a seat cushion, the rounded, broken plank of a wooden hull. The remnants of a shipwreck. Had she washed up from that same boat?

The man followed her gaze. "A tropical storm came in suddenly last night," he said.

She rubbed the goosebumps on her arms that persisted despite the heat and wondered how long she'd been in the water.

"Rose," the man said. "Tell me what happened." He squatted beside her.

She took in his appearance for the first time. He had short black hair, tan skin, and stubbles from not having shaved for some days. He was lean and muscular, especially his legs, like someone who ran or hiked frequently. She thought she read kindness and intelligence in his eyes, though that might've been her wishing it to be so.

The man had called her Rose and she supposed that must be her name, because she couldn't remember any other. She had no clue who he was, but since he knew her and had saved her from drowning, she wondered if he might be her boyfriend or even her husband. That would explain why her skin warmed to his touch.

Chapter Two

KAILEY

CAN anyone be trusted to narrate their own life? Not me, that's for sure. My feelings influence how I remember things. My anger, fears, and disappointments cast a shadow over everything. What about the positive emotions? I don't recall a lot of those growing up.

But there's no one else to tell my tale, so here I go for what it's worth. Don't worry, I'm not going to spend a lot of time on my early years. Who really wants to hear about anyone else's childhood? Walking at one, potty-trained at two, stealing the neighbor kid's bike at three. It was downhill from there.

I'm not going to pin everything on my being fatherless, though it's tempting. I'm aware plenty of people grow up just fine with only a mom or a dad, or with two moms or two dads. Still, what a ready excuse the single parent thing could be for all my failures. Shoplifting from H&M: *no dad*. Flunking biology: *no dad*. Smoking weed: *no dad*. I could have my own theme song, like in *The Wizard of Oz*: "If I only had a brain… a heart… the nerve." *If I only had a dad*.

Whenever I tried to pin Mom down about him, she acted like it was a virgin birth. News alert, Mom: I knew how children were born by the time I was seven. Finally, after years of my begging her to tell me, she said she didn't know who he was. That gave me a brief flash of hope as I pictured a *Mamma Mia!* scenario with three cool older men, any of whom might be my dad, and in the end I could pick the one I liked best. But then I remembered this was my mother we were talking about, and it was hard to imagine one cool guy dating her, let alone three. Eventually I decided I was probably the result of a one-night stand, and Mom neglected to get the man's full name, phone number, or address to track him down later.

But I've had a lot of time to think about my mother (and everything else) since then, and I no longer believe she was that careless. She's one of the most meticulous people I know when it comes to doing anything. No way would she screw a guy without collecting all his vital information. Which meant the reason I had never met my father was that he didn't know I existed. Mom didn't tell him because she's a control freak. My dad would've wanted to have a say in my upbringing, and she had to make sure that never happened.

I'll tell you about one incident that will give you an idea what Mom was like. Every year, she brought me to the county fair. They had an indoor facility where local people showcased their collections. Along with the usual boring stuff—baseball cards, bottle caps, PEZ candy dispensers—they always had a few that were incredibly weird. One time someone brought condiment packs, you know, like ketchup, mustard, and soy sauce. Another year there was a collection of barf bags. Seriously, barf bags.

Mom's thing was dolls. Yeah, this is what I'm talking about, she was an adult fixated on dolls. I wasn't allowed to play with them, which was fine with me, because I never liked them anyway. She filled our apartment with Barbies, American Girls, baby dolls, and even trolls. It was creepy as hell. I felt like they were staring at me all the time, and probably doing sinister things while I slept. But Mom was like a doll herself, with her perfect hair and the way she always put on her lipstick with two sharp points at the top. With her clothes that had flawless color coordination and never any wrinkles. I liked being messy, but when she still had a say in the matter, she wouldn't let me out of the house until she'd made me look like a miniature version of herself.

At the fair I wanted to go on the carnival rides... I *dreamed* of going on a carnival ride. I begged Mom to let me do it. Sometimes she said it was too dangerous; other times she said the spinning would make my little tummy ache. Really, that's the way she used to talk to me. She also called me "K-K."

When I was six, Mom and I were standing near the ride I wanted to go on more than any other—the airplanes. It so happened one of the women who judged the collections every year noticed Mom and stopped to talk with her. I saw my chance and asked in my sweetest voice if I could go on the ride. Sweetness had no effect on Mom, but I thought it might impress the judge. Sure enough, Mom was about to say no as usual, but then she stopped because she didn't want to look like a mean mother in front of this lady.

I was bouncing up and down with excitement when I got into my own little plane and the bar was closed over me. The planes started moving and soon we were flying over everyone's head. I had a wheel and I'm pretty sure I thought I was really steering the thing. It was the happiest day of my life so far, and still ranks up there with my best, as there haven't been too many of those. I couldn't stop smiling as the plane went round and round, weaving up and down. I'd never been in a real airplane, but the idea of flying had always filled my imagination. With the wind on my face, I pictured myself soaring like a bird.

The ride began to slow down way too soon. I wanted to keep going for a few more hours. The plane eased to a stop but I still sat there, hoping no one would notice me and I could continue flying around.

"K-K, come here!" Mom shouted. Just my luck, the lady she wanted to impress had gone away.

The attendant, a skinny boy with a nose piercing, came over, raised the bar, and told me I'd have to get in line again. I made sure not to look at Mom as I walked around the other way back toward the line. It made me cringe to hear Mom scurrying up behind me.

"I called you," she said.

I actually started running, but she was faster and caught up with me right away, grasping my shoulder from behind.

I whirled around. "I want to go again!" I said.

Here's one of those places where my narration gets sketchy. The way I remember it, at this point Mom looked exactly like the Wicked Witch of the West. No broomstick or bicycle, just a long green face with eyes of flint.

"I told you one time only," Mom said. She didn't cackle, but she might as well have. *I'll get you, my pretty.*

"Please, Mommy. *Please.*" Thinking back, I'm amazed she didn't manage to terrify me into silence, but it goes to show how badly I wanted this thing.

Mom took my hand and squeezed it so hard, tears came to my eyes. "I said no. Mommy knows best. We're going inside. I think the judging started." She pulled me away. I tugged on my hair—a habit I've always had when I get upset or anxious—

and stared back at the planes, just starting to rise up into the air again. *If I only had a dad.*

I know things could've been much worse. This isn't an excuse for what happened later. It's just the way things were, that's all.

Chapter Three

ROSE

WHEN ROSE WAS strong enough to stand, the man took her arm and led her over the crest of a low hill to a cabin that had been built on scrub grass, next to a small shed and a generator that hummed. She still wasn't ready to talk and the man respected that.

As soon as they entered the cabin, he got her a towel and showed her a box that held some women's clothing and a pair of sandals. She took the T-shirt, pair of shorts, panties, and bra closest to the top. *Do these belong to me?* she wondered. They looked like the right sizes, but she wouldn't know for certain until she tried them on.

"You can rinse off in the washroom. There's clean towels on the shelf," he said. "I'll make you a sandwich."

She felt comfortable inside his little cabin and wondered if that was because she had been living here. Not that anyone could stay in such an isolated place for very long, but maybe they had come here on some sort of holiday. It was clean and uncluttered and brightly lit by sunshine. There was a corner kitchen with a propane stove and a refrigerator. A compact table with one chair, a recliner, a bookshelf, and a single bed occupied the rest of the space.

The single bed puzzled her. If they had come here together, wouldn't they at least have asked for a double? One of many mysteries to address in time, but certainly not the most important.

She went into the bathroom, which had only a basin, small tub, and water tank. No toilet. The shed outside must've been the outhouse. At least she hoped so, as the alternative would be squatting among the trees. She shut the door, and when she turned back, she was drawn to her reflection in the mirror over the basin. The face that stared back at her evoked no memories. She might as well have been looking at a stranger. *At least I'm a pretty stranger.* As quickly as the thought occurred, she berated herself for being shallow.

Rose—who needed to remind herself the man had said that was her name—had hazel eyes, long auburn hair, and a narrow face with clear skin except for a light mole on one of her cheeks. Probably she was in her late-twenties but it could've been plus or minus five years. Her eyebrows were brown and smooth. Her nose was straight and a bit pointed at the tip. Her lips just seemed normal, not too full or too thin. Her teeth were aligned in the perfect way that can only be achieved by braces. There was nothing particularly arresting about her face, but altogether the features formed a pleasing picture, she thought.

She drew back her hair to examine the tattoo on her neck. It was like an animation of a bird swooping up into flight. Five representations of the same bird as it went from perching to soaring with open wings. Though she wasn't certain what she thought of tattoos in general, she liked this one. She also liked that it had no color; the image was inked in shades of grey.

Rose could not recall anything about this tattoo or what had prompted her to get it. But that wasn't surprising, because she couldn't remember a single thing about herself, not her name, or where she grew up, or what she did for a living. Whether she had a husband (who might be the man, but she wasn't sure) or children, living parents or siblings, dear friends or grandparents... she had no idea. At the same time, her head teemed with information. She could recite facts about famous people, dead and alive. Facts about history, politics, science, technology, art, and culture. She could remember the titles and plots of countless films, and details about the actors who starred in them.

She slipped off her sundress and panties and looked down at herself. Her skin was pale, her body slender and attractive, she supposed. Her feet had been bare when she washed up onto the beach. She wore no polish on her finger- and toenails, and had no piercings, which somehow relieved her, she didn't really know why.

Rose stepped into the tub and turned on the faucet. The water that emerged from the hand sprayer was slightly warmer than the room temperature. She washed her hair, soaped all over, and rinsed off. It felt good to dry herself with the thick towel and to put on the clean clothes. She used his comb to remove the tangles from her hair.

When she came out of the bathroom, the man looked at her. "Lunch is ready," he said.

"Thank you." These were the first words she'd said to him, at least since she'd lost her memory. He smiled.

As she crossed the room to the table, she had the urge to touch everything. The firm wooden walls, the soft, thin curtains, the smooth window glass, the fluffy quilt on the bed. It wasn't enough to look at these things, she had to feel them as well. She didn't know why the touch reassured her so much.

The man got out a second folding chair from the closet and set it across from the other one at the table. He'd assembled matching sandwiches with sliced turkey, cheese, lettuce, tomato, and onion on whole wheat bread. Rose wondered where he could've gotten the ingredients—was there a supermarket, *through the jungle and right at the creek*? But she was too hungry to worry about it at the moment. As soon as she sat down, she lifted her sandwich and took a huge, glorious bite. Tomato juice dripped down her chin, but she didn't care. She hadn't ever tasted anything so good before. *Or had she?* One more thing she didn't know.

His eyes shone with amusement watching her eat. She devoured her meal quickly and ravenously, and then drained her glass of water. She wiped her lips and chin, satisfied now, and wondering how she would tell her boyfriend or husband she had no idea who he was.

"I can't remember anything," she said at last, resolving to begin with the more general explanation of the problem.

He paused chewing to stare at her. "Anything?"

She waited to let that sink in.

"You mean about the shipwreck?" he said.

"Well, that… and everything else."

"At least you know who you are, right?"

"I don't." She took a deep breath. "Not even my own name. You called me Rose. Otherwise I wouldn't know."

"Wow. Okay." He thought for a moment. "Do you remember me?"

She touched his hand, and there was that electricity again. "I'm so sorry," she said. "I'm sure it has nothing to do with my feelings for you."

"Feelings?" he said.

"Yes, I mean, I'm sure my feelings are the same." If only she could remember what they were.

The man laughed. "What do you think our relationship is?"

Why is he making this so difficult? "That's what I'm trying to tell you. I don't know if we're a couple or not."

He laughed harder. Rose drew back her hand, annoyed.

"Sorry," he said. "It's just... I only met you two weeks ago. I don't even know your last name."

"What?" she said. It was all so horribly confusing.

"You were with another research group on the island. You, another woman, one man. We met briefly after I arrived. The three of you left on the sailboat yesterday."

"So you and I...?"

"Barely know each other," he said.

"Where is this place?" Rose got up. "How far are we from civilization?" She stared out the open door.

"A thousand miles to Hawaii, give or take a hundred," he said. "Whitaker Island. Pacific waters all around us."

"We're both American?" she said. "We sound American."

"I am. And I just assumed you were. Unless you're Canadian. Say the word, 'a-b-o-u-t.'"

"About?" She pronounced the second syllable with an 'ow' sound.

"Probably not Canadian," he said.

"Who else lives on this island?"

"It's just us at the moment."

She wrapped a tress of her hair around her finger and pulled on it. Things were worse than she'd thought. Much worse.

He stood and shook her free hand. "Let's try this again. My name is Thomas Blackburn. I work in environmental research. You do too. Your name is Rose. I'm pleased to meet you. I'm sorry to say I know nothing else about you."

She watched the ocean in the distance. "You said I left in a sailboat with two other people," she said. "They must know who I am."

Thomas frowned. "Yeah," he said. "But only you came back."

Chapter Four

KAILEY

THE THING about control freaks is their behavior works against the very thing they're trying to achieve. I mean, if Mom had let me have my way now and then, I might not have been so determined to break away from her. But there was no compromise in her world. Either I obeyed or I was punished. Vindictively punished too. One time she took a dress—my favorite white halter—and cut it to shreds with a pair of scissors. She didn't like to be crossed.

But her predictability made her easier to deceive. I knew she had no respect for my privacy. I knew she would search my room whenever I was out of the house. I knew she would monitor everything I did online. Knowing this... expecting it... allowed me to keep one step ahead of her.

I learned deception at an early age. I became an accomplished liar, forger, and thief. A master of concealment. I avoided confrontation, because I knew from past experience I would never win an argument with her. She was skilled at twisting everything I said, so that I always came out looking like a demon, and her, a saint.

Which was why I never told her about the scholarship. It was the best day of my life, even better than the airplane ride, when I got the email telling me I won. I never won anything else, before or after. It's not that I was a terrible student. Okay, I was terrible in science, but in everything else, my grades were average. Mom said I should just get used to it, and that no one in our family ever did well in school. Book-learning wasn't all that important, according to her. She was a hairdresser, so I guess it wasn't essential to her job. For a while I thought I'd be a hairdresser too, after I finished high school.

But when I found out about the scholarship, I knew I had to try for it, even though I expected to fail. Filling out that application was the most effort I ever put into anything. I got Sean to look it over, but he didn't change much. He told me to trust myself—that was something I never heard before. He said my passion came through and that was generally what people were looking for when it came to doling out scholarships.

And he was right. I was selected, along with three other kids my age. We all came from different high schools in the Bay Area. The day I got the notification, I had to keep reminding myself not to grin like an idiot. Nothing made Mom more suspicious than unmotivated happiness.

The day before the first class, I gave all my weed to Jenna and Sean. That's how much I cared about this. It wasn't just because I heard there might be a drug test required before I could get my license. I was about to receive professional training, and therefore I must rise to the occasion and become a professional myself. No weed, no beer, no drugs of any kind. *Safety first.*

The next morning, I rode a bus to the San Carlos airport. It was late coming, which made me wish I'd arrived sooner to catch the earlier bus, even though the longer I stayed out, the more suspicious Mom would become about what I was doing. Luckily, my friend Jenna was great at sounding like an adult. She would pretend to be her own mother. I'd tell Mom I was going to Jenna's house, and when she called to check up on me, my friend would put on that voice and convince her I was in good hands and not to worry.

When I finally reached the airport, Mr. Cho was already there with the other scholarship kids. I spotted them on the tarmac next to a beautiful Cessna 162 Skycatcher, and hurried across the parking lot toward them.

I thought something must be wrong when Mr. Cho saw me approaching and moved away from the others to intercept me. The serious expression on his face made me start tugging at my hair. When he reached me, he spoke quietly so the others wouldn't hear. "Didn't your mother tell you?" His tone was more concerned than angry. He was a nice man, Mr. Cho.

But as soon as I heard him, my stomach twisted inside and I felt like I was going to throw up. I think I said, "what?" or "gaaa," or maybe I just gaped at him. Usually I did a better job covering, but this was something I really cared about.

"She called us," Mr. Cho said. "She told me she didn't sign the permission form."

I struggled to pull myself together and blank out my feelings the way I usually did. "She did sign it," I said. "You saw it. She forgets stuff like that."

"She told us you forged it." His tone was stiff now. He'd been willing to sympathize until I started lying.

I was probably as young as nine when I began practicing her signature. After years of her volunteering to chaperone on field trips and treating me like I was five years younger than whatever my age was, I began signing the forms myself, just so she wouldn't find out. One time another mother told her the class had gone to the pumpkin patch, and she realized what I'd done. For punishment she locked me in my room every day after school until Christmas break. Of course, I still kept forging stuff. But I became more selective about it.

I was going to keep lying to Mr. Cho, because that was what I did, but he interrupted. "Don't," he said. "Lying just makes things worse. I'm afraid we can't award you the scholarship. You're only fifteen. She has to approve it."

"But I... I can't afford flight training without it."

"I'm sorry, Kailey. My hands are tied. Maybe if you talked to her?"

If I hadn't been so miserable, I would've laughed. This was a woman who hadn't wanted me to ride a toy airplane. She would tie me up and lock me in my room forever before she'd let me pilot a real one.

My hopes and dreams drained out of me that day and vaporized like water on the hot tarmac.

Chapter Five

ROSE

"DO you think the others died in the shipwreck?" Rose asked.

"I don't know," Thomas said. "Maybe they're somewhere else on the island."

"We should look for them."

"If you're strong enough."

"I think I am." She looked down at her feet, thinking she ought to wear the sandals that were in the box, when a noise began outside... an ear-grating whistle, unlike anything one would expect to hear on a deserted island in the middle of the Pacific.

She and Thomas exchanged a baffled look, and then Rose was out the door, with Thomas just behind her. They squinted upwards at what looked like a small jet or rocket, trailed by a billowy gray line of exhaust. It made a thunderous *neeeyowww* as it plummeted, disappearing behind trees before exploding on landing. The sounds of wrenching, twisting metal followed, while black smoke spiraled upwards to the sky.

They both stood frozen for a moment. It flashed into Rose's mind that this must be the Bermuda Triangle of the Pacific. First a shipwreck, now this. *What will be next?*

Thomas was the first to move. He rushed back into the cabin, looking for something. Rose went after him to see what he would do. He found his backpack and loaded it with a first-aid kit and a few water bottles.

"What else do we need?" Rose said.

"You're coming?" he said.

"Of course." She didn't like the skeptical look he gave her, as if he saw her as a poor, frail thing who couldn't walk ten steps without resting. Actually, she felt strong and thought she'd rather be moving than sitting and waiting in the cabin.

Thomas retrieved a hatchet from the closet.

"What's that for?" Rose said.

"Cutting and hacking." He headed outside without waiting for more questions.

Cutting the seatbelt off a trapped pilot? Hacking through the jungle? Rose supposed that was what he meant. "Wait!" she called out, rushing to the clothing box. She slipped her feet into the sandals and pulled the straps up behind her heels. A perfect fit. They had to be her clothes, even though it didn't make sense they were here in Thomas's cabin, given that he didn't even really know her.

Outside, she found Thomas waiting at the edge of the jungle. He led the way toward a trail that went roughly in the direction of the crash.

"Were you expecting a plane?" she said.

"No. If I was, it would've been a seaplane."

Thomas had on hiking boots and could move faster that

Rose in her sandals. She took running steps behind him to keep up.

"Why would it crash out here in the middle of nowhere? In good weather," Rose said.

"I can't say."

The narrow trail wound upwards. The growth was thick around them, and the ground slick with heavy moisture. Rose slid backwards on the mud, grabbing onto a branch to keep from falling.

"Careful," Thomas said.

There was no point in asking him about the jet or whatever it was. He didn't know any more about it than she did. They would find out more when they reached it, if the pilot or any passengers were still alive.

"Tell me about the other two scientists," she said. "What were their names?"

"Dave and Samantha. And no, I don't know their last names either," he said. "I didn't expect to see any of you much. We were busy, doing our own work. I figured I'd get to know you all in time."

Their first names did not spark anything inside her. No memories of what they looked like, or how she felt about them, or what they did together. "I wish I could remember them," she said. "Were we close?" A horrible thought occurred to her. "Were Dave and I a couple?"

Thomas snorted. "Couldn't you just be single?"

"I was only wondering!" In fact, despite how attractive he was, Rose was beginning to be glad she wasn't married to Thomas, who could be infuriating at times.

"The three of you were co-workers. You'd been here for several months studying invasive species on the island. My impression was you were going home to your own families."

She was confused. "But we left in a boat... I don't get why

we left in a boat. Couldn't we call for a seaplane? Were we trying to make it to Hawaii? Wouldn't that take a long time?"

"Three or four days? I don't really know."

"Didn't we know a storm was coming in? Didn't any of us have the sense to check the weather?"

"It's complicated," Thomas said. He stepped up his pace and it was all Rose could do to keep up with him.

Chapter Six

KAILEY

I WAVED my hand above my head, making sexy astronaut Barbie fly across the starlit sky.

"What do girls like about dolls?" Noah asked.

"They can take any shit you fling at them," I said.

"How do you know?"

"Look at her smile. Whatever you do, you can't take her happiness away." For years I felt like all the stupid dolls at Mom's house were staring at me with their cold, judgmental eyes. Sometimes when I got angry at Mom, I took one of her Barbies and banged its head like a hammer on the tile floor in the bathroom. Now and then I cracked the head and there was hell to pay for it. But no matter what I did to meter-maid Barbie or surgeon Barbie or deep-sea-diver Barbie, that smile never went away. It made me envy them even more. *Do your worst, Mom.* Whatever you do, you can't take my happiness away.

But she could.

I put Barbie back in the paper bag. She was in great condition—just as if a child had never been allowed to play with her—and might be worth something. This morning I'd stolen her from an estate sale. I waited until a woman with a walker started to haggle with the owner over the price of a side table. The owner claimed it was an antique, but the woman wanted some kind of proof, like a letter from *Antiques Roadshow*, I guess. In the meantime, I took astronaut Barbie and slipped her into my bag. Then I checked my phone and pretended a message had just arrived calling me away, lol. *As if I was a person in demand.*

Noah and I lay on our sleeping bags in Golden Gate Park. It was a rare warm night in San Francisco, when we didn't actually need to be covered. For once it wasn't the worst thing being homeless, except for having no shower. I pushed my greasy hair back from my forehead. I kept it short now, so it wouldn't bother me as much when I had to go for days without washing it.

Noah was hyped up about something tonight. I used to like it when he got like that, until I realized it only happened when he had an idea. And the idea always involved me in something I wasn't sure I wanted to do.

"I used to play soccer with this dude, Kevin," Noah said. "He thinks he's the bomb, but he don't know shit. Always bragging about his grandfather's classic Hot Wheels collection."

"Yeah? That's gotta be worth a lot." Thanks to Mom, I was well-aware of all the useless things people collected, and how much others were willing to pay for them.

"Grandpa lives in San Mateo," said Noah. "Alone in a fucking mansion."

An old man by himself. Something small and specific to steal. It might not be so bad. "I guess we could sell the cars at auction," I said. "Nobody would know."

"We're gonna need a gun," Noah said.

I tensed up inside. "You know how I feel about that," I said. I must've told him a thousand times. Stealing was one thing; violence another.

"No bullets. We show him the gun so he lets us in." Noah rolled on his side to look at me. He reached over and touched my cheek. "I checked out his place. He sets his alarm system when he leaves the house. And probably when he goes to bed, like eight o'clock."

I didn't say anything. I knew I should tell him I didn't want to bring a gun, even if it was unloaded. But it was hard to say no to him. He'd rescued me from a freak who tried to get me addicted to heroin. I could trust Noah to look out for me. He said he loved me and I believed him.

"Your mom still have that semi-automatic?" He said it casually, like he might say, *your mom still have that chocolate cake?*

That was it, of course. I'd been stupid enough to tell him about it. Later I realized he would never give up until I got it for him.

I touched my neck. Three weeks earlier, on my nineteenth birthday, I got a tattoo of five small, graceful birds overlapping each other, so that it looked like one single bird opening its wings and taking off in flight. I didn't tell Noah because I thought he wouldn't want me to spend the money. To my surprise, he liked it. He didn't complain about the money, but he did use it as an excuse to get me to steal more often. *If only you hadn't spent everything you had on that tattoo...*

It was healed now. And whenever I put my hand on it, I liked to close my eyes and picture myself as that bird, soaring up into the air and leaving my troubles behind.

I've complained a lot about Mom, and Noah has plenty to answer for, but in the end we make our own choices, don't we? I have no one to blame but myself for the train wreck I made of my life.

Chapter Seven

ROSE

AN HOUR MUST'VE PASSED before Rose and Thomas grew close to the crash site. During that time, the trail narrowed and nearly disappeared. Thomas used his hatchet frequently to clear the way. It was best to stay well behind him, while he swung the sharp blade about. In any case, she could not keep up with him.

Following the stench of smoldering undergrowth, and the glimpse of smoke, Thomas turned off from the trail and began clearing a path toward the crash site. Rose thought he might've picked this spot because of the unusual tree growing there, with bright red, spiky flowers shaped like scrub brushes. It would help mark their way back.

The hacking required to get through the vegetation slowed their progress. But at least they didn't have far to go before reaching the blackened clearing where the jet had crashed down. Nothing appeared to be burning any longer, probably because the jungle growth was too full of moisture to catch fire.

The jet or whatever it was loomed ahead of them. As Rose stared at it, feelings of curiosity, awe, and fear rose inside her. The craft was built of sleek, black metal, but it was bent and twisted, with one of the two short, thin wings broken off. It did not look as if anyone could've survived the impact.

Thomas shot a glance at Rose before approaching the wreckage. She hurried after him, and they both paused near the nose of the craft.

"Hello!" shouted Rose. "Anyone in there?" No response came. She hadn't really expected one.

So close to the hull, she now noticed strange markings on one section of it. There were several rows of shapes... circles within circles, bisected by lines at various angles. It made her think of a drawing by Paul Klee, though it seemed strange for a manufacturer to etch artwork into the surface of their aircraft.

Overall, she had never seen anything like this jet before. There were no windows, nor anything that resembled a cockpit. No visible doorway or hatch. The more she thought about it, the more she became convinced this must be some sort of top-secret new military design. Maybe it crashed because it was still being developed and they hadn't worked out all the kinks.

"What're you doing?!" she shouted at Thomas, who had just pulled himself onto the one wing that was still attached. The craft rocked dangerously. "What if it's a missile?" she added.

Thomas was calm. "It would've exploded on impact," he said. He craned his head upwards. "There's an opening on the top." He paused, frowning in thought. It looked like some new idea occurred to him as he scanned the area of the wreckage. He jumped down from the wing and ran to the other side of the craft.

Rose, baffled, called after him. "What're you looking for?"

"Not sure," he shouted back.

She was sick of following him about. Approaching the wing, she wondered if she could climb up and get in through the top to see if anyone was alive in there. She had thought Thomas was going to do that, but he obviously had some other idea that he refused to share with her.

She climbed easily onto the jet. The smooth-looking metal provided better traction than she would've expected. It felt more like some kind of plastic than metal, and yet not really like plastic. Again, she wondered if this were an experimental aircraft, made of some newly invented material.

She reached up from the wing to the top of the craft and was able to grip the edge of the opening there. She pulled herself up to the top and peered in through the hole.

It was one large open space, the cockpit she supposed. There were no seats, only long black tendril-like straps that hung down from the ceiling. Flat, gray panels with the same kind of markings she'd seen on the outside of the craft were set into the walls.

No one was inside the jet, and she wondered if there had been a pilot at all. Probably it was self-guided. That was a reassuring thought. It made her feel better to believe no one had been killed.

She started to pull her body up, to lower herself into the cockpit or whatever it was.

"Rose, get down!" Thomas shouted.

"There's no one inside," she said. "I'll just take a look around."

"GET DOWN! You don't know how the controls work. You might touch something accidentally and who knows what will happen. You might activate a weapon."

She hesitated. Strangely, when she tried, she could actually picture the cockpit of a jet inside her brain. But this didn't look anything like it. She didn't know how the panels functioned. It was possible she might press a switch that would do something unexpected.

"Fine," she said. But it was annoying having him tell her what to do all the time.

She slid back down. Thomas caught her and helped her back to the ground. She liked the feel of his arms around her, but he let go quickly.

"We need to leave," he said. His tone held a new urgency that filled her with foreboding. "First I need to show you something."

He led her away from the wreckage to the edge of the crash site. A large, black *mass* of some sort was heaped on the ground. As they drew closer, needles prickled inside her. She didn't believe in premonitions—so far as she knew—but if she had believed in them, this would've been a good time to turn and run.

She held herself together, pulling on her hair as she stared down at this thing, whatever it was. If she had to give it a word, she would've called it a cocoon. It was woven of the same black tendrils she'd seen inside the ship. It was hollow inside, but its walls looked thick and protective. It had an opening in the center, where, if it were a cocoon, the "moth" would've emerged. But it would have to be a giant moth indeed, because the space was sufficient to hold a creature much larger than a person.

"What do you think it is?" she said, though she wasn't sure she wanted to know the answer.

"I think…" he said. "I think the thing that was in the spaceship ejected out of it wrapped in this." He pushed the hair back from his forehead. "And now it's gone."

"Thing?" she said.

Chapter Eight

KAILEY

WHILE STANDING in the hall waiting for Mom to answer my knock, I realized I should've gotten a copy made of my house key before she took it away. Epic fail on my part; I underestimated her desire to get me out of her life. Now she might look through the peephole and just pretend not to be home.

But I guess I caught her on a good day, because she opened the door only a minute or so later. Naturally she was holding Monica in her arms. If she didn't, the cat would try to shoot past her legs to freedom. Monica had succeeded a few times before, only to be cornered downstairs in the lobby. She was a mean cat, but I couldn't help root for her. She was smart enough to know that living under Mom's dictatorial rule wasn't worth the guarantee of one measly meal a day.

"Hi," I said. I learned long ago, the less I spoke, the more likely I could avoid turning an encounter with Mom into an all-out confrontation, complete with hissing, spitting, and claws coming out.

She gave me a suspicious look and blocked my way. "What brings you here?" she said.

I raised the paper bag. "Need your help with this." I pushed past her into the apartment. Mom shut the door and let Monica down. The cat shot into Mom's bedroom, where she would go into the closet and bury herself under Mom's sweaters on the shelf. I never understood why Mom doted on her, when Monica clearly had no desire to spend even a second in the company of human beings.

I took Astronaut Barbie from the bag and handed it over. "Worth anything?" I said.

"Not much without the packaging." Still, she looked her over carefully, taking off her clothes so we got to gaze at the full unanatomical glory of her. "Where'd you get her?"

"Estate sale," I said. That much was true.

Mom probably guessed I didn't pay for her, but she knew I'd never admit to it, so there wasn't any point in bringing it up. She took the doll with her into the collection room, aka my former bedroom. I followed, pausing at the doorway. The room grew more disturbing by the day, ever since Mom quit her job as a stylist at Great Clips and became a full-time buyer and seller of vintage dolls. My old room had been transformed into an office slash shipping center slash storage warehouse. My old bed was gone, replaced by a desk, and the walls were now lined with shelves. Barbie dolls, American Girls, baby dolls, trolls, action figures, bobbleheads and more filled every available space. I held back a shiver.

Mom sat at her desk and began to look up astronaut Barbie on her computer.

"Gotta pee," I said. I went down the hall, but instead of going to the bathroom, I slipped into my mother's bedroom. I went straight to the dresser and opened the top drawer. The pistol was underneath her undies, as it had been for two years since the break-in. No one was home at the time, and all the thief got was her laptop and a few dollars, but the very idea of someone violating her carefully maintained personal space was so upsetting, she went straight out and bought a weapon. She didn't know how to use it and didn't own any bullets, but she must've thought that simply waving it in an intruder's face would get them to go away, if she was home the next time it happened.

I wish I could say I hesitated to put the Glock in my bag. I wish I could say I thought long and hard about the implications of taking this gun. That I considered what would happen if Noah did, after all, buy some bullets. That I reminded myself the weapon could be traceable to my mother, and therefore, to me. If I had stopped to think about any of that, maybe things would've turned out different.

But since I'd already decided I was going to do what Noah had told me to do, I kept my mind blissfully empty as I slid the gun into my bag and tiptoed out. I went into the bathroom, closed the door quietly, and flushed the toilet after a minute. I turned on the water to pretend I was washing my hands, because Mom would be sure to notice if she didn't hear running water after a flush. I looked at my oily hair and wished I could stay and take a shower, but I knew I ought to get out of there right away. Mom would search my bag if she got half a chance.

"Gotta go," I said as I opened the front door. "I'll check in later."

Mom dashed into the hall and snapped up Monica as she sprinted from the bedroom toward the slim chance of escape. The cat let out a yowl of frustration. *Blocked again.*

Chapter Nine

ROSE

THOMAS SET a brisk pace for the return trip, even faster than he had gone on the way up the hill. All Rose could do was trot after him. One time she skidded, fell, and muddied her dress. He paused to give her a hand up but continued on immediately after.

"We have to go to the beach," Rose said as they neared the cabin.

"Why?" said Thomas, without stopping.

"What if Samantha or Dan reached shore like I did? They might need our help."

"Dave," he said.

"Okay, Dave." She couldn't help that her memory was gone.

Thomas paused and changed direction. "You're right. But let's be quick."

It was high tide at the beach. The sea covered any evidence of the shipwreck that she'd seen earlier.

Thomas scanned the shoreline. "There's no one," he said.

"Wait," said Rose. She ran down the beach, her eyes on the water in case a body might be bobbing near the surface. But she found no signs of anyone. When she paused to catch her breath, however, she wondered if she saw movement next to the largest palm tree at the far end of the shore. She squinted, but the shape was indistinct. It frustrated her not to see clearly, and she suddenly wondered if she might be nearsighted. She turned her gaze back to Thomas, who looked small and vague in the distance. When she glanced once more at the tree, there no longer appeared to be anything beside it. She stared for a few more seconds, reassuring herself that it had only been shadows shifting in the breeze. Still, her heartbeat quickened as she set off at a jog toward Thomas.

"Any luck?" he said.

She shook her head and they hurried back to the cabin. By the time they reached it, the sun had disappeared, leaving the sky sprayed with the colors of dusk.

Inside, Thomas fetched nails, a hammer, and a stepladder from the closet. "Can you take the flashlight?" he said.

Rose hesitated before picking it up and following him out. Things were happening so fast, it was hard to keep up. Thomas led her to the first window, where he began working with hurried movements and frequent furtive glances toward the deepening shadows of the jungle.

"Shine the light on me?" he said.

She obliged while he closed and latched the storm shutters.

"Will you talk to me?" she said. "Do you really think there's some sort of... alien... loose on the island? I don't understand why you're so quick to jump to crazy conclusions."

He paused to look at her. "There's stuff you don't know.

We'll talk about it soon, I promise. But right now, we need to move quickly."

He set up the ladder and proceeded to nail the first shutter in place.

"You're scaring me," Rose said.

Thomas glanced around and whistled. "Brandy!" he called out. "Brandy, c'mere girl!"

"Who's Brandy?" Rose said.

"My dog. I haven't seen her since this morning. She does like to wander, but she should've been back by now. She might be lost."

Rose didn't care about Thomas's dog. She didn't know, or couldn't remember, what it felt like to have a pet. "Do you think that jet or whatever it is could be from China? Or North Korea?" she said.

"Let's finish here," said Thomas. "We'll talk inside." He moved the ladder to the next window. Rose followed with the flashlight.

The cabin was dark when they went back in. Rose kept the flashlight on until Thomas had bolted the door and lit three oil lamps.

"All these preparations... I don't get it," she said.

He turned back to her. "Why do you think you and your friends sailed off in the boat? A boat that really wasn't meant for a thousand-mile trip. Operated by people who didn't know much about sailing."

"I assumed we came here that way." She perched on the edge of the recliner while he paced.

"You came by seaplane. Same as me. The boat was meant for use around the island. The U.S. Fish & Wildlife Service owns it."

"Where's the seaplane?"

"Fish & Wildlife owns that too. They send it if anyone

needs to leave the island."

"Why didn't we call for it?"

"Our communications died."

Communications. Of course. Why hadn't she thought of that earlier? She peered around the cabin and spotted a laptop on the shelf.

"Have you tried connecting today?" she said. "We should call for help. Someone could be searching for my friends out there." Precious time had been lost. Why hadn't Thomas done anything?

"I've been checking every few hours for days. It's no good."

"What *is* your communications system?" It occurred to her it must be tough to get a signal in the middle of nowhere.

"I've got a box and an antenna on the roof that connect me to Inmarsat, a global satellite system."

"And you're screwed if that stops working?"

"No," he said. "There's another facility on the other side of the island. Where you and the others were staying. It has its own system, and a backup in case there's a problem. We tried all three. Nothing."

"How could that be?" she said. "Unless… the satellite is dead?"

Thomas took the advanced-looking laptop from the shelf and set it on the table. "I need to show you something. You'll understand then."

"You have electricity, right? I saw the generator."

"Yeah." Thomas entered a password and launched a video, then stood aside so Rose could watch it.

A newscaster addressed the camera, his face drawn and anxious. "Astronomers at the Jet Propulsion Laboratory have confirmed the approach of a spacecraft of alien origin," he said. An image replaced the newscaster: an enormous black spherical object looming in space.

"So far, they've been unable to establish a line of communication," the man continued. "Scientists and engineers from around the globe are working to——" The screen went blank.

"We lost the transmission then," said Thomas. "There hasn't been anything since."

Rose clicked to replay the video. She paused on the image of the spaceship. It looked more like a planet than a transport vehicle, except it was oval instead of fully rounded, and the surface showed no variation in color or texture.

"An alien spaceship," she murmured. She hadn't actually believed the rocket they'd found could be from outer space. She wouldn't have believed this news report either, without the other, physical evidence. Images were too easy to fake these days.

Thomas was leaning against the counter, watching her.

She looked at the ceiling, picturing the spaceship hovering above them like a malevolent Death Star. She squeezed her arms around herself.

"After we saw the broadcast, we were skeptical. Was it some kind of prank? Maybe a hacker was behind it. But then when we lost our signal, and still didn't have it back after a week, we figured it must be true. That's when the three of you decided to leave."

"I'm surprised you didn't come with us."

"You all wanted to get back to your families. But for me, this seemed like the safest place. An island in the middle of nowhere. I could wait until everything got sorted out." He gave a bitter laugh. "Then what do you know?" His hands mimicked an explosion. "Phoom! A goddamn alien ship crashes down right here. And something gets out of it."

Rose's shoulders tightened. She wished he wouldn't talk like that. He made it sound so monstrous.

Chapter Ten

KAILEY

WHEN WE'D STOLEN BEFORE, it was always taking advantage of an opportunity. Shoplifting when the clerk wasn't paying attention. Seeing the door of a house or garage left open and running in to grab the nearest thing that might be worth something.

This was different. We targeted the house based on Noah's information. We knew what we were going to take. If the collection was decent, it could net us at least a few thousand at auction. Hot Wheels weren't like fine art, where you needed papers showing where you got them. Nobody had receipts for toys their parents bought them when they were kids.

We had gone to the neighborhood the night before. It was a nice home in the suburbs, not a mansion like Noah said, but big compared to some other places. The best thing was, it had a long driveway and a bunch of trees to hide behind. We snuck up near the house to watch for a while. Eventually the lights went off downstairs and came on in an upstairs bedroom. The room had an open window, which we figured wasn't wired because you couldn't reach it without a ladder. A minute later, we heard five short beeps that must've been the old man entering the code for the alarm system.

The next day, we took the train down from San Francisco in the late afternoon and walked from the station. It was a couple miles, not too bad. We didn't have much money to spend on Ubers, plus then there would be a record of us being in the area. Noah wore a baseball cap and had grown a beard just for this. I was glad he'd be shaving it off tomorrow. I wore a button shirt and khakis, and a hijab so people would think I was Muslim. Hopefully that would be all they remembered about me.

But the closer we got to the house, the more anxious I got. I would've been tugging on my hair, but the hijab got in the way. When we were nearly there, I said, "Maybe we shouldn't do this, Noah."

"What're you talking about?" he said.

"What if we get caught?" My voice sounded higher than it usually did. "I don't want to go to jail."

"We won't get caught."

"You don't know that."

Noah stopped and grabbed me by the arm. "You owe me this. I took you in when you ran away."

"Took me in? We live on the street."

"I got you away from that fucking pimp," he said. "I taught you to survive."

He did do that. I was grateful for it. But I wondered how long I'd be paying him back, and whether the price would just keep on rising.

His voice softened the way it did when he wanted to talk

me into something. "So do this one thing for me. We'll be good after this. We just need some cash to get started."

I began to think it would be okay. Just this one job and we'd be set.

"We'll take the money and fly to LA," he said.

Fly to LA, I thought. "That's right. I want to learn to fly."

"You never been on a plane?"

"I mean, get my pilot's license. I wanted it since I was fifteen. Mom wouldn't let me."

Noah laughed. "I can't picture you flying a fucking plane."

It's hard to admit this part, even to myself. Now was the moment I straightened my shoulders and resolved to go through with the robbery. It wasn't friendship or loyalty or love —definitely not love—or any of the finer emotions that motivated me. Nope. It was having something to prove. No matter what it took, I would show Noah I could *fly a fucking plane.*

As we approached the entrance, Noah hid and I took the padded envelope that I was "delivering." I whipped off the hijab and shoved it into my purse before I rang the doorbell.

"Who is it?" the old man said through the door.

"Amazon delivery," I said. We figured that on any one day, probably ninety percent of the population was expecting an Amazon delivery. Plus an old man might forget whether he'd ordered anything or not.

He was quiet for a minute and I started to get worried. What if he was calling the cops? But then I saw the knob turning. This was when I was supposed to throw on my ski mask, but the door came open too fast, and the old man looked right at me.

His gaze shifted to the driveway and he looked confused, probably because there was no delivery van or even just a car. I thought he was about to shut us out, so I stuck my foot in the house and leaned against the door. Noah ran forward wearing his ski mask and gloves, with a bag in one hand, the gun in the other. "We're coming in," he said. "Do what we say and you'll be fine."

The old man blanched and backed away from the door. He was a thin, short Asian man. Asian-American, as we found out later. He was wearing a T-shirt, yoga pants, and no shoes. I suppose we had just interrupted his exercise routine.

"Please don't hurt me," he said. His frightened eyes reminded me of a Chihuahua I'd seen at the park not long ago. The poor little dog had cowered when his owner raised his hand like he was going to hit him. It broke my heart to see that.

"Get your mask," Noah hissed at me, angry.

I got it out and put it on. My gloves too. The old man had seen me, but only briefly. It was okay, I told myself. He wouldn't remember what I looked like.

I followed Noah in and shut the door.

"Where's the kitchen?" Noah said.

The old man was trembling and didn't respond—probably too scared to say anything. Noah grabbed his shoulder, turned him around, and shoved him forward. The man fell into a table in the hall, and knocked over a China trinket, I think it was a ballerina of all things. The trinket shattered on the stone floor. The man looked down at it and started to weep. I don't know why, but it flashed into my mind that the ballerina probably had been a favorite of his dead wife's.

Now is when my memory starts to get hazy. We were still in the hall… and I know there was a mirror because I stared at the reflection for a moment that felt frozen in time. It was a horrifying image of two terrorists in ski masks, one of them looming over a helpless old man and pointing a gun at his head. The old man whimpered, overcome by grief and fear. The terrorists frightened me too, even though I was one of them.

I used to see myself as the victim, bullied by others, my mother most of all. But I couldn't deny the evidence of the mirror. I was the bad guy, the bully, the brutish invader. *What happened to me?*

Noah dragged him to the kitchen and I shuffled after them, reluctant and ashamed, though not enough to stand up to Noah. I duct-taped the old man to the chair according to our plan, while Noah held the gun on him. The old man was shaking so bad I was afraid he might have a heart attack.

I could tell you this was when I swore never to threaten an innocent person again. But promises are cheap, and while I felt strongly about it at the time, I can't guarantee I would've kept this one. All I can say is it struck me as a crucial point in my life, where I could continue down the path to *hell-and-damnation* (as Mom would've said), or I could turn back. I just don't know if good intentions would've been enough to wrench me around.

The old man didn't hesitate to tell Noah where the Hot Wheels collection was. No question he was praying we'd take it and leave as fast as possible. After he gave his answer, Noah made me duct-tape his mouth. Tears ran down the old man's cheeks while I did it. Noah went off to find the car collection, and I waited with the prisoner. It was supposed to be my job to watch him, but I tugged at a handful of my hair and stood with my back to him, because I couldn't bear to look at what I'd done.

It seemed like a long time before Noah returned with his bag full of Hot Wheels, though it probably was no more than five minutes. He waved me into the hall.

"We should leave one at a time," he said quietly.

That hadn't been part of the plan, but I was so anxious to get out of there and not have to look at the old man anymore, I didn't question what he was saying. *Still thinking of myself.* I raced out the front door, and Noah shut it behind me. I yanked off the itchy mask and started to take off my gloves. But it gnawed at me, Noah telling me to go ahead. Then all at once I knew what it meant, and the realization took away my breath and made me choke for air. I turned back and clawed for the knob to open the door.

BLAM! A shot went off inside the house. I cried out and clapped my hands over my mouth. I bent over, arms clenched around my stomach, moaning. I'm not sure how long I stayed like that. When I could move again, instead of going inside, I turned and bolted like the coward I was. When I reached the street, I tried to calm down, tried to look like I was running for exercise, even though I wasn't dressed for jogging. I kept it up all the way to the train station. Somehow I managed not to bawl. My head was crammed with thoughts about getting on a bus, going somewhere, anywhere else, leaving Noah behind forever. To this day, I'm not sure why I didn't do it. *Fear of the unknown* would be my guess.

So when I got to the station, I sat on the bench to wait for him. A train came while I was waiting, and I considered throwing myself in front of it, but it was just too horrible to picture my mangled body. After the train left, I was the only one left at the station, and that's how it was when Noah arrived ten minutes later.

When he walked over, I got up and shoved him sideways, not onto the train tracks like I probably should have. "You said you wouldn't hurt him!" I said. "You said no bullets!"

"He saw you."

"Just for a second!"

"I couldn't risk it," he said.

"Fuck you, Noah!" I said. "I never should've trusted you!"

He wrapped his arms around me. I cried hysterically and tried to push him away. He kept his arms tight over me.

"It's okay," he said. "Everything's gonna be okay. We'll sell the shit, make some money, go to LA. I'm gonna take care of you." He kissed my hair. "I love you, baby."

I buried my face against his shoulder. I didn't really believe any of it: that we would make money or go to LA, that he loved me, least of all, that everything would be okay. But Noah was all I had in the world, and I didn't know what I would do if I lost him. *Fear of the unknown,* all over again.

Chapter Eleven

ROSE

A SURREAL, uneasy atmosphere descended over the room. Rose and Thomas had done all they could by nailing down the shutters and bolting the door. It would not have made sense to go out after dark, searching for something that might or might not be on the island. It was still possible the spacecraft had been piloted automatically, and there hadn't been any alien inside at all. Without more information, all they could do was hunker down and hope they would be safe here, at least for the night. In the morning they would have to decide their next steps, because they couldn't stay locked inside the cabin forever.

Thomas had proposed dinner. Rose figured that like most men, he couldn't manage without three meals a day, and snacks. But she had to admit the aroma of spaghetti sauce cooking in a pan over the gas burner was reawakening her own appetite.

She had cleaned up and changed out of her muddy clothes while he was cooking. It distracted her to put on a pretty sundress, a white one with purple lilacs. She admired herself in the mirror before coming out of the washroom.

"Did you say these were my clothes?" she said. It seemed like too much of a coincidence that everything, including the sandals, fit just right.

"Yeah," he said. "There wasn't room for them on the boat. You handed me the box right before leaving. I brought them back here not really knowing what to do with them."

She sat on the comfortable chair and watched Thomas's back while he chopped vegetables for a salad. Oddly, the movement of his shoulder blades under his shirt stirred something inside her. At the same time, he seemed unfamiliar and she wasn't sure if she trusted him. He made her think of a wild leopard on the savannah, all grace and power, with a dash of danger.

What did she really know about him? Only what he'd told her, because she had no memory of her own. Even the few things she now "knew" about herself came from him. Her name and why she'd been on the island and how she came to wash back up on it.

Even if she had her memory back, she would hardly know anything about him. Apparently, he'd barely spoken to her. What did she know of his life back in the states, and his motive for coming alone to this island? How many scientists went off to do research in a remote location without any companions? It seemed strange and unusual.

And yet here she was, about to spend the night alone with him in this tiny house, with the windows nailed shut and the door locked. Her instincts told her this was a bad idea. But the alternative of going out *there* and taking her chances against a possible alien wandering about in the darkness, was naturally out of the question.

The way the lamps cast flickering shadows against the walls did nothing to soothe her. "Why don't you have electric lights?" she said. "You have a generator."

He let out a small laugh. "I like it this way."

Her gaze wandered to Thomas's laptop. It was the latest design, extremely slim with a display that expanded as needed to create a wider screen. "Can I use your computer?" she said.

He began peeling a carrot and spoke without turning back. "I'd rather you didn't. Got my whole life on there. Not sure I'm ready to share."

"I wouldn't look at your personal files."

"You might without realizing. My organization sucks."

His answer was lame but there was no point in insisting at the moment. "Okay," she said. She leaned back and reached for a book from the shelf. She looked at its title in surprise.

"Seriously?" she said. "You brought *Robinson Crusoe?*"

"It was meant to be a joke," he said. "Who's laughing now?"

She flipped through it without really looking at it. She was thinking about how she needed to get off this island. Whether or not there were aliens swarming the earth… whether or not they were friendly… she couldn't stay here. She needed medical attention. A doctor ought to be able to help her get over her amnesia.

But what if she couldn't be cured? What if she had a husband, parents, children who were looking for her right now? Or worse… what if her loved ones had died in an alien attack on the mainland?

The U.S. Fish & Wildlife Service must have records of who she was. If the memories didn't return, she could still find out.

They would have an address for her. The name of an emergency contact. She would go there. If she could find her home or family, surely something familiar would trigger her memories to return.

She glanced up from the book she wasn't reading and noticed a second box under the bed. "Is that mine too?" she asked.

"What?" Thomas said.

"The other box under the bed. Is that more of my stuff?"

"No, it's mine," he said.

It seemed odd that he didn't say what was in the box. *Oh, that's my rock collection*, or *those are my candy bars*. Most people would just naturally come out with whatever it was. Unless they wanted to keep it a secret.

"Time to eat." Thomas gestured for her to come sit. The salad and spaghetti were already set out on the table.

"Thank you," she said. It seemed natural to be polite. She must've had a good upbringing, she thought. Or perhaps her parents had been strict with her.

"Where did you get the vegetables?" she said.

"There's a garden. I'm sort of barely maintaining it," he said. He passed her the spaghetti, which was topped with a vegetarian tomato sauce. She put a medium helping on her plate and waited for him to help himself before starting.

"Salad?" he said.

"I'll take some later." She lifted her fork and began eating.

"How is it?" he said.

She paused. Really thinking about the bite in her mouth. "Amazing," she said. "It tastes so good. You must be an excellent cook."

"You were probably starving. That makes anything taste better."

She didn't know. She couldn't remember what anything else tasted like, or what her favorite foods were. All she knew was that his spaghetti gave her great pleasure, and she wondered that people did not eat it all day, every day.

"You said you were a researcher," she said. "What do you study?"

"The effects of pollution on sea life. But I don't think anyone will worry about that anymore."

"Why not?"

"Well, you know... aliens?"

The reminder made her aware of the noises coming from outside. The wind had picked up. Branches creaked and air whistled through the cracks around the door.

"Do you think they might be friendly?" she said.

"If you just wanted to reach out and make friends in a non-intimidating sort of way, why would you arrive in an enormous ship? It's like if the pilgrims came to America in the Titanic... assuming the Titanic could've made it across the Atlantic."

"The Starship Enterprise had a crew of a thousand," Rose said. "And their mission was exploration." It was disconcerting to know more about Captain Jean-Luc Picard, and the android Data, than she did about herself.

"So they said. But they fought a lot of battles for being all about nonintervention. And the alien ship has room for way more than a thousand. Way more."

"I suppose it depends how big they are," she said.

"If they're all the size of Godzilla, just kill me now."

"What do you think their plan is?"

"Take Earth for themselves," Thomas said.

"If so, wouldn't they want to keep our plant life, ecology, oceans, atmosphere? If they didn't want those things, they could've gone to Mars and had it all to themselves. Here, if they don't want to share with us, they'll have to wipe us out. That could turn the planet into a wasteland."

"Maybe they have ways of killing us without setting off

bombs. Gas if they don't mind exterminating all animals. Well-targeted lasers. Mind control. I don't know."

Rose lowered her fork. The thought of so much destruction made her uncomfortable.

"Let's face it, we know nothing about them or their motives," Thomas said. "Maybe they like to hunt and kill and eat their prey. Maybe that's why they're here." He looked at Rose and must've realized he'd gone too far from the distress reflected in her face. "Sorry." He returned to eating his spaghetti.

The thought of being consumed as prey was enough to take away Rose's appetite, despite how good the food tasted. Her stomach felt tight even though she hadn't eaten very much.

That was when it happened. The sound began quietly. At first, she thought it was only branches scraping against each other. But as the volume grew, the quality of the sound stretched and twisted until it became a wail. A chilling, other-worldly wail.

Rose gripped the table. She turned her head sharply to look behind her, though there was no way the alien could be there. The door and windows were in the other direction.

Thomas seemed frozen in place. His mouth hung open as he stared at her. A deep silence followed the wail, as if it had compelled all the other creatures of the island to go still, for fear the monster might hear them.

Then Thomas got up. He checked the bolt on the door and made sure the windows were locked even though they also had the wooden shutters nailed over them.

It happened again. Another wail like the first, except it lasted longer, its sickening refrain drawn out, invading Rose's pores. She grasped her hair and pulled on it. Thomas, too, was fixed in place, with one arm still raised to the window. Was this how the creature captured its prey? Its sound rendered the victim immobile until it could be devoured? Like a snake's venom…

"Jesus," Thomas said at last. His voice conveyed the dread she felt.

"It's terrifying," Rose said, though it wasn't something that needed saying. She felt the need to get up now, to walk even if she could only cross from one wall to the other. "What are we going to do? We can't just sit here and do nothing." She was aware of an hysterical tinge to her tone.

"Better than going out there," Thomas said. "At least we have this building between it and us."

"Is that really enough?" She could swear that when the beast cried out the second time, it was closer.

Chapter Twelve

KAILEY

AFTER THE MURDER, Noah decided he better not try to sell the stolen cars too soon. I thought he was showing some regret over what he did, but not for the right reasons. It finally dawned on him, the cops don't put a ton of effort into solving burglaries. But as soon as you add a corpse into the mix, it moves to the top of their to-do list.

We found out most of this later at the trial, but the first thing that happened, was Noah's old soccer teammate—the one who told Noah about his grandfather's Hot Wheels collection—went straight to the cops. When he found out what was taken, he thought over everyone who knew about the collection, and the one that stuck in his mind as *most-likely-to-commit-a-crime* was Noah. *What do you know?* He had also heard Noah was homeless and living in the park.

He must've given the cops a great description because they

found Noah pretty fast and—with us not having a clue—an undercover guy started following him around. The second thing to happen was Mom realizing her gun was missing and reporting it to the cops. You can be sure she knew who took it, but she wasn't the type of mother to deal with it by talking to me directly. She always took the path that would cause me the most pain, embarrassment, and trouble. Like when she called the flight instructor ten minutes before my first class was about to begin, so I'd be sure to show up and suffer the ultimate humiliation.

The cops got even more interested in Noah after learning his girlfriend's mother was missing a gun, and probably doubled up on their surveillance after that. It didn't take long for Noah to go back to the cheap storage locker in Daly City where he kept the few things he owned, like his drum set from high school that he was probably never going to use again because he wasn't very good. After the cops followed him to the locker, they got a warrant, opened it up, and found the Hot Wheels and the gun. *Yeah, the gun.* Noah was that stupid. I'm sure he thought he'd get a chance to use it again someday.

Even the crickets had gone to sleep by the time they showed up to arrest us that night. I'll never forget waking to their voices. "Freeze! SFPD! Stay down!" We both did stay down, but that didn't keep the officers from jumping on us and wrenching our hands behind our backs, while another cop read us our Miranda Rights. They cuffed us and practically dragged us back to the patrol cars. I had plenty of scrapes and bruises afterwards.

That was the last time I saw Noah until my trial. As soon as we got to the station, they separated us and brought me to an interrogation room. Detective Pine, the little prick, kept the spotlight on me, and refused to give me water or anything else. After a while, he let me call Mom, but she just hung up on me.

The detective didn't break me though. He kept saying they had enough evidence to prove we did it. He told me he knew Noah was the one who shot the old man, but it would make everything a whole lot easier if I would just confirm it. He offered me a plea bargain, I'd serve time for the robbery, that was it. All I had to do was rat on Noah. Juries always had sympathy for the girl, he said. They figured the man bullied her into it.

"I don't know anything about it," I kept saying. "We didn't do it."

Later after I got my court-appointed attorney, she also urged me to confess. "Noah will get the plea bargain if you don't," she said.

Noah and I had talked about what we'd do in this situation. We knew they'd try to play us against each other. Hell, it's in every episode of every lawyer show on TV. But if we stayed strong and neither one of us confessed, it would be hard for them to get a conviction. There were no witnesses, no fingerprints. We'd worn gloves. The case was based on circumstantial evidence. I just had to say nothing, and Noah would make up a story about an enemy that wanted to frame him, who planted that stuff in his locker. The story only had to be good enough to create reasonable doubt.

I wasn't as stupid as it sounds at the moment. I knew there was a strong chance Noah would betray me. I knew I ought to confess. *Why didn't I?* A perverted sense of honor, I guess. If I couldn't keep the sworn promise made to my lover, who was I? I might as well have pulled that trigger.

"It was her mother's gun," Noah said from the witness stand during the first day of my trial. "I didn't know she brought it until... Mr. Lee saw her face when she rang the doorbell. That's why she shot him."

Although I knew at that point that he would testify against

me, it still shocked me to hear the lies coming out of his mouth. I thought he wouldn't be able to look me in the eyes while he threw me under the bus, but he did. His lawyer probably coached him, told him the jury wouldn't believe him if he couldn't look at me. So he managed it.

But what hurt the most—what skewered me in the back and right on through my heart—was finding out my fingerprints—*only mine*—were on the Glock. Noah had told me he wiped it off. *So clean you could stir your grandmother's tea with it,* he'd said. That was a big fat lie, since I never touched the thing after sticking it in his backpack for him. *Just put it there, I'll clean the prints later,* he'd said. Of course, he made sure not to touch it himself until he had the gloves on. My prints were his insurance in case we got caught. And it worked. His testimony slipped the noose over my head, but the evidence of the fingerprints tightened it round my neck and sent me swinging from the tree.

The verdict was no surprise to anyone, least of all me. I sat there numbly as the forewoman shouted, "Guilty!" Maybe she didn't actually shout, though that's how I remember it. The word echoed in my head for months afterwards. *Guilty. Guilty. Guilty.*

When it came time for sentencing, Mr. Lee's daughter addressed the court. "My mother died when I was thirteen... my father raised me and my two brothers."

The lawyer had advised me not to show too much emotion, but I couldn't help my eyes filling with tears.

"He worked at Mills Hospital," the daughter continued. "Cared deeply about other people. Volunteered as a Visiting Angel." She had to pause to settle herself and wipe her eyes with a tissue. "My daughter is getting married in three weeks. Her grandfather was going to lead her down the aisle. It breaks all our hearts. She..." here the daughter looked straight at me,

"...robbed him of this joy... robbed his family of his loving presence."

The judge delivered his line after that: "The court sentences you to life in prison without parole."

I kept thinking about *The Shawshank Redemption* as they transported me to prison and checked me in. Not the good part, you know what I mean. What I pictured was the torture, both physical and mental, that happened after Andy first arrived at the prison gates. I kept thinking how, like me, he was innocent of murder. But not being guilty did jack shit for him.

A guard led me into a dorm filled with beds separated into cubicles. A crowd of female inmates watched. In my paranoia-infused mind, they looked like giant, vicious hawks with their hungry eyes fixed on me. Ready to rip and shred their next meal with their knife-edged beaks and needlelike talons. *I was that meal.*

Chapter Thirteen

ROSE

"DO YOU HAVE A GUN?" Rose said.

"A gun?" Thomas looked at her in surprise.

"Did you hear that sound? It was beastly. We have to defend ourselves." It left her with a feeling like ants crawling over her. She wanted to scrape them away, but it was impossible.

"I'm a poor excuse for an American. No guns." He went to the utility closet and got out the hatchet they'd taken into the jungle. He threw it down on the table. "Just this," he said.

Rose removed it from its sheath and looked over the blade. It was nicked and blunt from hacking through branches. "Can you throw it?"

"I can throw anything. The question is, can I hit the target?"

"Well can you?"

"Probably not."

"If you don't know how to throw it, you'll have to get close to the creature to use it," she said. She looked toward the kitchen, thinking. There were knives in the butcher block. She got up and took out two long ones. "Do you have any sticks?"

"I'd rather have the hatchet."

"No, I mean..." She went to the utility closet and got out a mop and broom. She searched a little more for duct tape. "We can make spears," she said.

Thomas grabbed a screwdriver. They sat and began urgently constructing their spears, unscrewing the mop and broom sections first.

"What's on this island, besides us?" Rose said.

"What do you mean?"

"I mean, animals."

"Bats... birds... mice and rats... I don't know. Not much."

"What about wild boars?" she said.

He shook his head. "There's nothing big."

"Meaning we're the biggest animals here."

"That's right," he said. "And Brandy." He looked nervously at the window. "Shit. Brandy."

"If that alien is as big as it sounds," Rose said, "and if it's hungry... it's coming after us."

"It doesn't know where we are."

"They came from another planet. They had a lot of time to observe us. They must know we live in houses. And it can probably smell us." She wasn't sure why that was the scariest thought of all. Maybe because there was no way of knowing if the alien had sniffed them already and was tracking the scent. Her hands grew clammy as the image of a giant ant-like creature flashed into her brain, although she recognized it as the creation of a B-movie called *Them!*

"Maybe we should talk about something else," Thomas said. He got a pair of scissors to cut the duct tape.

"Fine," she said. "Why don't you tell me everything you know about me?"

"I've already done that."

"All you said was my name. And what my group was working on."

"That's all I know. I haven't been here that long," he said. "Just a couple of weeks. And only the first week was normal."

"But you must've spoken to her. I mean, me," she said. It was hard to think of the woman she was before she lost her memory in the first person.

"Not really. I didn't think there was any rush to get to know you. Figured it would happen in time. Then after we got the news, your group started making plans for the trip to Hawaii. Practice runs in the boat. Loading up supplies. You weren't hanging out here trying to make friends."

"Okay," she said. His explanation did make sense. "You don't know anything about me. What about yourself? Why did you come here alone?"

"I told you, I've been studying—"

"I mean, why do you live here *alone*?"

"Oh, you mean... *alone*."

"You don't have a wife or a girlfriend or a boyfriend," she said.

"Not into guys."

"You're still not answering the question." She was starting to notice he was good at that.

"I was married for a while," he said. "It didn't work out."

"Did you cheat on her?"

"No! Why would you ask that?" he said.

"A lot of guys cheat," she said. "Or so I've heard." She had no experience of relationships that she could remember, but she knew from books and the news that men often had affairs.

"You seem to know a lot for someone with no memory."

"I do know a lot. I know all about the world. I know about science, culture, history, technology, the arts, and all sorts of things. But I don't know about me. Did your wife cheat on you?" she said.

"There was no cheating on either side."

"Then how did it not work out?"

"She died," he said. "That's what happened. She died."

That took her by surprise. Thomas looked like he was in his mid-30s. He was young for losing a wife. "How did she die?"

"Do we really have to talk about this now?"

"Not if you don't want to."

"I don't."

"Did she have cancer?" Rose couldn't help herself. Curiosity was such a strong emotion. At the moment, she felt overwhelmed by it. Had she always been so curious about everything?

"You don't give up, do you?" he said.

She didn't know how to answer that, because she didn't know if it was normal for her to be persistent or not.

"She wasn't sick," Thomas said. "She didn't have an accident either. She was murdered."

"Did you murder her?" The words slipped from her lips before she could stop them. She regretted it, watching his face transform with disbelief. But she couldn't take the words back now.

"Wow." He stood up and turned away from her, like he was feeling actual, physical pain. "Really? No, I didn't murder her. I loved her."

"I'm sorry," she said. She had crossed a line she should not have crossed. Then she tried to justify it. "I asked because, according to statistics, the husband is the most likely person to murder a woman."

"Well not in this case."

"Do you feel guilty? You know, because you weren't able to protect her?" She didn't mean that as any sort of accusation. It was just curiosity again. She honestly wondered how he felt about the whole thing. How it had affected his life. She wondered how she would feel if she had a husband and he was murdered. Depending on the situation, she might feel responsible.

"I think you must've had another career back in the states," he said. "Sociologist. Or psychiatrist."

She thought about that for a moment. It could explain why she was so curious about feelings. But when she looked at Thomas, she wondered if he was laughing at her. "Are you making fun of me?"

"No, I really think that might've been your profession at some point."

It was true she was having a hard time not thinking about Thomas and his wife. "I bet you're punishing yourself," she said. "That's why you came here. You don't think you deserve another woman, because you let down the first one. At least, in your own eyes."

"Seriously?"

She wasn't sure why he was annoyed. These were only words. If he didn't agree, that was fine. It was nothing but talk. "Can I see a picture of her?" she said.

"I think we're done."

"I'd like to see what she looked like."

"Why?"

"I'm sad about what happened to her. I might feel better if I can see a picture of her during happier times." That was true.

But she was also curious to see what sort of woman was attractive to Thomas.

"I apologize if the tragic and unnecessary death of my wife made you sad."

Rose wondered if Thomas's heavy use of sarcasm was related to his guilt over his wife's death. But she decided there was no point in saying that. She reached across the table and touched his computer. "You must have some pictures in here," she said.

"Leave it alone." His voice was calm but there was an edge to it.

Rose drew back her hand. "I didn't mean to upset you."

"It's okay. Just a sensitive topic."

She wondered how much he could've loved her if he didn't keep photos of her around anymore. She thought he did have photos. The issue was his computer. There was something on it that he didn't want her to see. And that made her want to see it all the more.

Chapter Fourteen

KAILEY

THEY EVENTUALLY SENT me to Second Chance Women's Correctional Facility in Manteca. This was one of the new private prisons they built because of overcrowding in the public system. No one wanted to end up here. We all knew private prison guards wrote up at least twice as many disciplinary reports as public prison guards. *Why?* Parole boards deny inmates with a history of behaving badly. The inmates serve more time, and Second Chance gets a second chance to earn more money. We lifers were sticking around in any case, but the guards didn't spare us when they went around dishing out reports like they were hand wipes. It would've looked suspicious otherwise.

People can get used to almost anything. By the end of two years, I'd grown into a dreary acceptance of my life. A lot of bad shit took place in the first year and a half, but I don't want to dredge it up as it has no bearing on what happened later. I'll just say, when you're the new kid in jail, it's like running a gauntlet. The prize if you make it to the end is that the other inmates leave you alone.

I learned to keep to myself because I decided it doesn't pay to have friends. Friends expect favors, like when they want you to pick up the drugs that their contacts on the outside fling over the fence. Yeah, stuff actually gets thrown over the fence without guards noticing. Or sometimes the guards are in on it.

Having friends also makes you part of a group, and if you're part of a group, you can be sure there's another group that doesn't like your group. Then you're stuck having to defend your group against the other group, when you never even wanted to be part of a group in the first place. I had enough of that crap in high school.

So I spent most of my time working on the factory line, assembling duty gear accessories for police officers. Like hand-cuff cases, personal protective equipment pouches, mag light holders, radio holders. Ironic, no? Inside prison we manufacture the tools cops will use to put us back here, if we ever get out and return to a life of crime. The work is boring as hell, but I needed some way of making money to buy the eyeliner and chocolate that helped make me feel as if I was still a human being. Mom never sent any money. The last time I saw her was the day I went home and stole her gun. She probably had officially disowned me, for all I knew.

In those days I had two roommates. Helen was at least fifty, and Bridget was younger than me. We weren't friends but we respected each other's space. There had been four of us in two bunks until Frankie died of an infection or some other thing they probably could've cured if they'd treated her fast enough, and then I got to move into the lower bunk, thank god. That may sound heartless, but Frankie was a lifer and a schizophrenic evangelical Christian. Some days she'd shower us with M&Ms she bought in the commissary, thinking all this niceness and praying and Bible-reading would net her a ticket through the pearly gates. Other times, she'd lie in bed glowering at everyone, gripped by despair over her crimes being too horrific to ever be forgiven, and haunted by the devil's open arms. I didn't believe in either place, but I was quite sure she'd never feel pain or misery again, and that wasn't a bad thing.

I think the first time I saw Paul—or Pall, as I thought of him, for the way he cast a pall over everything—was the same day I stared down into my bologna soup at lunch and saw it as a metaphor for my whole sorry life. One lone chunk of gray meat floated in gray broth. Like me—a blend of damaged parts that never added up to a pleasing whole—bobbing blindly about in a hostile, foul-smelling sea. That was the state of my mind at the time.

He was watching me when I returned my tray. The new guard. A big man with small eyes under spiky caterpillar brows. He had greased-back hair, fleshy lips, and a weird chinstrap beard that connected his sideburns. I knew better than to make eye contact with him, but out of my peripheral vision I could tell he was staring at me in a way that made my leg muscles tighten. Every instinct told me to run. Except when you're in prison, there's no place to hide.

I sped up as I passed him, but I wasn't quick enough.

"What's your name?" he said.

His voice slithered into my pores and caused sweat to break out. I had to stop because of what he could do to me if I didn't. He walked in front of me, but I kept my gaze lowered. "Kailey," I said in a weak voice. In retrospect, I should've lifted my face and barked out my name. Tormentors seek out the weak, like wild cats stalking their prey.

"I'm the new guy," he said. "You can call me Paul."

Pall, I thought.

"Don't walk so fast," he said. "It looks as if you have somewhere to go." He laughed as if he really thought that would be funny to someone sentenced to a lifetime of fetid gray soup.

"Yes, sir," I said.

"I said call me Paul."

I nodded. Luckily a food fight broke out in the cafeteria, and he had to go deal with it. I scurried away with relief.

I'm not certain about the rest of the day, but most likely I went outside to do my usual run in the yard, round and round the perimeter for an hour. Some of the other inmates had taken to calling me Gumpie, because I reminded them of *Forest Gump.* Maybe I had that same straight-backed posture as I pictured Forest's epic cross-country run and imagined how amazing it would be to somehow vaporize through the fence and then just keep on running on the other side, across Central Valley, up the Sierra Mountains, and down again to the wide-open Nevada desert.

I would've gone to the factory after that, and then for dinner I most likely ate noodles from the commissary. I'm sure I couldn't face more bobbing bologna or any other of the disgusting gray meat boiled up every night, impossible to tell whether it was beef or chicken or rat.

At last I reached the time I looked forward to every day. Second Chance had one good thing going for it: handing out Kindles to whoever wanted one. But you did have to pay for the e-books unless they were in the public domain. Meaning I only started reading Charles Dickens because his books were free. I began with *Oliver Twist,* because I'd heard of it. I loved how Dickens' writing transported me away from the miserable reality of Second Chance Women's Correctional Facility, into another time and place—although I did picture Noah as the wicked Bill Sykes. I identified with Oliver, and then Nancy. Her ending was tragic, but Oliver's brought proof that there's kindness in the world. It made me feel hope, though not for myself, because I obviously wasn't going anywhere. Hope for humankind, I guess.

That night I was going to continue *A Tale of Two Cities*, which I'd started the night before. *It was the best of times, it was the worst of times...* it made me think of schizophrenic Frankie who had died. Helen was asleep and Bridget not yet back from wherever she went after dinner, when I got out my Kindle from under my bed. I had used a good deal of my precious cash to buy a cover for it. When I opened it, I was surprised to find a scrap of paper tucked inside. I unfolded it and read, "YOUR SEXY AS HELL, I WANT TO DO U."

The hair rose on the back of my neck. A lot of the inmates were lesbians (or *gay for the stay*), and a few had hit on me in the past. But this was a new level of creepiness. I tore the note into tiny pieces and threw it away. After that I didn't feel much like reading. I lay back down and tried to sleep.

Later a footstep woke me. I looked up to see Pall standing at the entrance to our cubicle, staring down at me. I closed my eyes quickly and pulled the blanket up over my face.

"Everything okay over there?" another guard called out.

I heard Pall walk away. "Just beautiful," he said.

That was the beginning.

Chapter Fifteen

ROSE

ROSE PICKED up a throw blanket from a hook and wrapped it around her shoulders. She wasn't sure why she needed it, since the air was warm, but somehow it comforted her. "I would share information about my life if I could," she said.

"I appreciate that," said Thomas.

Considering how she might find out more about herself, she remembered the box of her possessions on the floor. Rose picked it up and dumped its contents on the bed. "Maybe there's a clue in here."

She sifted through the clothing but nothing else was there. Then it occurred to her she might learn something from the items themselves. She held up a pair of shorts: a simple style in muted colors. The other pairs were similar.

"I don't think I'm a very flamboyant person." She made a

separate pile of the underwear, which was all black or white or beige. "No wild colors here."

She raised two T-shirts in plain colors for Thomas to see. "Look at these," she said.

"What about them?" said Thomas.

"They look like something you'd wear." At the moment, he had on a white T-shirt and tan shorts.

"So you have good taste."

"Okay... but there's nothing distinct here. No pictures of someplace I've been. No advertisements for a product I've used. No favorite band or beer or whatever."

"Maybe you didn't want to be a walking advertisement," he said.

A new idea came to her. "Maybe I left a note or something in my pockets." With growing excitement, she checked the shorts and pants. When she found nothing, she sat back on the bed in frustration, staring at the heap of clothing.

She wondered if it was normal for the pockets to be so empty, they didn't even have bits of fuzz or dirt or sand inside them. Especially sand. How could you live on an island and not pick up a lot of sand in your clothing?

Rose lifted a bikini top to her nose and sniffed it. The fabric had that *just-came-out-of-the-plastic* smell. "You know what's weird?" she said.

"I wouldn't know where to start at the moment," Thomas said.

She ignored his reply, while acknowledging in her own mind that the list of weird things kept growing longer. "This stuff all seems brand new," she said. "How long did you say I'd been living on this island?"

"A few months, I think."

A sudden gust rattled the house. Rose let out a cry and sprang to her feet.

"It's okay. Just the wind," Thomas said.

She rubbed her arms. "I'm so on edge."

Thomas woke his computer up. "We need a distraction." He started some soft music playing. "This might help calm us."

Rose listened. The singer's voice was comforting. "Who is this?" she said.

Thomas shrugged. "I don't know. It's an indie folk playlist I found online."

"Nice." Her body swayed to the rhythm. "Let's call it the Big Bad Alien Blues." The music was already improving her mood. "Will you dance with me?"

"You want to dance?" he said.

"Why not? Though I might be bad at it."

"Getting my toes stepped on is the least of my worries." He reached for her hand and drew her into his arms.

The movement took her by surprise. She hadn't been prepared for how sweet a sensation it would be to have him hold her. Even though this wasn't the first time he made her feel something inside. She had a hyper-awareness of his body, and whenever he stood close to her, or brushed his arm against her, or when she got a whiff of his aftershave or deodorant or whatever that scent was, she experienced a weakness in her knees. Twice earlier she'd felt her face flush when he glanced at her. She wondered if she'd felt this way about him before her amnesia. But if so, why hadn't she tried harder to get to know him?

She turned her face away from him so he wouldn't notice the glow of her skin, and pressed her cheek against his shoulder.

After a moment, he told her she danced well. She did feel graceful in his arms. Maybe she did dance well, or he was just good at leading her. It was easy to match her movements to his.

They danced around the room. Thomas hummed a bit to the music, which made Rose smile because his voice was off-key.

"I like your arms around me," she said. Maybe that wasn't something she should've said. It sounded like she was coming on to him. But then she couldn't see the harm in that. They were a man and a woman alone on an island, and they liked each other. A quote from the era of hippies flashed suddenly into her mind. *If it feels good, it can't be bad.*

She paused to look up at him. "I feel incredibly alive."

"What do you mean?"

"It's as if I never felt anything before, and I'm experiencing everything for the first time, and it's very intense. The smell and taste and touch of things, the sensitivity to sounds and visions, the warm sensation that fills me with your arms around me. So many feelings all at once. Are they always so overwhelming?"

"I don't know. Maybe you've just forgotten."

"Forgotten what it is to be human?" she said.

Shadows flickered over Thomas's face. The darkness softened his eyes and lips and made her want to kiss him. She knew kissing was supposed to feel good, but she couldn't remember doing it with anyone. The thought made her feel sorry for herself. *Twenty-five (or thirty?) years old and never been kissed.* So far as she knew.

She looked up and pressed her mouth against his.

Chapter Sixteen

KAILEY

PALL'S STALKING CONTINUED. He stared at me whenever he thought no one was looking. Sometimes he ran his tongue around his lips, which made me want to puke. He left notes all the time, describing what he wanted to do to me in disgusting detail.

I wanted to turn him in. I started saving his notes to use against him, even though I knew how futile it was. As if they'd believe me when I said Pall wrote the notes. As if they'd bring in a handwriting expert to compare his penmanship. As if my complaints about *the-way-he-looked-at-me* would meet with anything but ridicule. *As if fish could walk.*

Anyway, there's no good place to hide things in a prison cell, or cubicle, in my case. Two weeks after I started storing the notes in an old soda can, the can disappeared. At least the notes stopped coming after that.

But then Pall started something worse, making me wish for the good old days when all he did was write notes. He found ways to brush up against me whenever we were walking in the same area. His arm would rub against my breast, or he'd squeeze a chunk of my ass. One afternoon in a crowded corridor, he slipped his fingers between my legs and groped my crotch. When I jumped and cried out, he turned to another guard and claimed he'd just pulled a gum wrapper out of my pocket. He opened his hand and sure enough, there was the wrapper.

Gum was forbidden because you could use it to make an impression of a key. If you managed to send it home, someone could make a matching key and smuggle it back to you. It was worse if they found you with the wrapper but no gum, because then it looked like you'd already done the deed and sent off your gum.

No one listened when I said the wrapper wasn't mine. I thought about telling the other guard about Pall's harassment… the notes, the touching, the looks. But it was *Callous-Alice*, as some of us called her, and she wouldn't believe me, or wouldn't give a shit if she did. Worse, Pall would know I ratted on him, and he would find new ways to make me suffer for it.

They took me away for a strip search to find the missing gum, like there would be any point in shoving gum up my private parts. Then they sent me to solitary.

Pall's message was clear. *Here's what you get if you cross me.*

Chapter Seventeen

ROSE

IT SURPRISED Rose when Thomas pulled back from her kiss. "You don't like it?" she said.

"I don't think it's a good idea."

His reply stung and she didn't know how to respond to it. Instead she sat down at the table, doing a poor job of masking her disappointment.

"Rose, it's not about you. You're very attractive. But this isn't the right time. We need to be alert."

She thought "attractive" sounded like such a bland word. Wallpaper is attractive. Still, he had a point. They needed to be listening to the sounds coming from outside. They had to be prepared to defend themselves. She picked up the spear she'd been working on and tested how firmly the knife was attached to the handle. It felt loose. She cut more tape and wrapped it around as tightly as she could. A feeling of constriction gripped her stomach again, as her attention focused back on the alien threat.

Thomas stopped the music and sat on the recliner.

"When I'm afraid, it makes me want to crawl out of my skin," Rose said.

He leaned back, watching her.

"What about you?" she said. "Have you ever been frightened before?"

"Many times."

"What were you most afraid of?"

"Alien creature ranks right up there."

"I mean, before tonight."

"Ella James," Thomas said.

She looked at him, confused. "What?"

"Ella James. My first real crush. I was petrified of asking her out."

"That doesn't sound very frightening to me." It was silly. Ella James was just a girl.

"It was to me," he said. "I hated that I'd have no control over the outcome. She would say yes, or she would say no, and there wasn't anything I could do to change that."

"What if she said no? What was the worst that could happen?"

"My self-esteem would be shattered. And when she inevitably told her girlfriends about it, I would be humiliated. I was certain no other girl would ever go out with me."

"I see," she said, and in a way, she did. She couldn't remember her own adolescence, and yet she knew, perhaps from reading about it, that everything that happened took on an aura of life or death. An adult would know that if Ella James refused to go out with him, there would be other women who would. But to a child, a rejection could mean the end of his world. The crushing of his self-esteem. "There was a lot riding on this one date," she said. "What was her answer?"

"I don't know," he said.

"What?"

"I didn't ask her. It was just too scary."

"I bet she was disappointed." Rose thought she would've been disappointed. She also thought she would've asked Thomas herself if she wanted to go out with him. But his story made her wonder how much grief could've been spared over the years if people weren't so afraid to talk to each other.

She thought about the alien. "What if there was a way to communicate with it?"

"You were ready to shoot it after you heard its voice," Thomas said. He went to the closet and began looking for something.

"I've been thinking about that," she said. "It's a horrible sound to us, but it might be normal speech for them. It makes me crazy when I hear it, but it's a gut feeling, it isn't logical."

"Unless you're a linguist, I'm not sure how you'll find a common language." He found what he was looking for—a knife sharpener—and sat at the table with it.

"Really? What about English? All this time they were flying across the galaxy, they could've mastered our languages."

"We don't know how much time it took them. Maybe they found a worm hole and got here in ten minutes." He started sharpening the blade on his spear.

"What if we offered it something?"

"I don't know. It might be like a bear. You give it a little food, then it wants more and more, until you're the only thing left to eat."

Hot anger coursed through her. "Stop being an ass!" she said. "There's a creature out there. I've never heard anything so fucking creepy before. Can you at least try to come up with a plan?"

Thomas put down his knife and looked at her calmly. "Hey. Sorry. You're right."

Her anger disappeared as fast as it had arisen. Rose didn't quite understand it. Where had that come from? She didn't believe she was one to lose her temper easily. She didn't think she usually used the f-word either. It almost felt like someone else speaking through her mouth. "I'm sorry too," she said. "I guess we're both under pressure."

She put another piece of duct tape on her spear. It didn't appear that you could have too much. At the same time, she realized what that growing urgency inside her was. "I have to go to the bathroom," she said, turning to Thomas.

He frowned. "I'll come with you. I mean, I'll wait outside."

"You think it's all right?"

"We haven't heard the creature in a while," he said.

"Yeah. It should be okay." But she didn't feel as if it was okay.

Thomas lifted his homemade spear. "Take the flashlight."

Rose picked it up and turned it on. She thought about bringing her spear, but it seemed like a lot of weaponry for a trip to the outhouse.

Thomas listened at the door. After a moment, he opened it slowly and peered outside. Tree branches and palm fronds swayed in the breeze. He looked around in all directions before turning back to Rose. "Let's go."

He went ahead and opened the door of the outhouse. She sprayed her light into the enclosure, checking the corners and even the ceiling. She thought the alien was probably too large to hide inside that small space, but they hadn't seen it yet and couldn't be sure exactly what its size or shape was. Thomas closed the door after her.

Rose's gaze shifted to the toilet, and suddenly she remembered there must be a pit or a tank or something underneath it. With a trembling hand, she raised the lid and aimed her flashlight down into the dark hole just long enough to see there wasn't anything except what one would expect.

A small shelf stood beside the toilet, with paper and wet wipes. She set the flashlight down, sat on the toilet, and looked around. The walls felt like they were closing in on her. *Nowhere to run when the monster comes.* Moisture beaded on her forehead and her fingers tingled. She struggled for breath. *What's happening to me?* She tried to hold it together, closing her eyes and telling herself to breathe slowly and deeply. Somehow she knew these were the steps needed to control a panic attack.

The tight space freaked her out. It felt like a coffin, the way she could reach out and touch the walls on all sides. Maybe she suffered from claustrophobia.

"Brandy… c'mere girl." Thomas's voice came from outside. He whistled lightly. "Brandy, c'mon!"

Rose's heart raced. *Why is he calling the dog?* The alien would hear him. How could he do that while she was vulnerable inside here?

She heard the sound of branches cracking. Thomas was quiet now. No way to tell if he was still out there... or if the monster had silently killed him and was waiting for her to come out.

Rose kept taking deep breaths and forcing the negative thoughts from her mind. She managed to finish peeing. She trembled as she pulled up her underwear and cleaned her hands with a wipe. "Thomas?" she whispered.

He didn't answer.

She picked up the flashlight, glad it was one of those heavy metal ones. If need be, she could strike the alien with it. If she got close enough before it struck her down.

"Thomas?" she repeated, standing by the door. Again, no reply.

She turned the knob slowly and paused. She raised the flashlight above her head, preparing to strike, and slowly opened the door.

Blackness greeted her. There was no sign of him. She felt like screaming, *you said you'd watch the door!* She peered into the dark jungle. The noises that came out of there were disturbing. Rustling branches, crackling undergrowth. The sounds that a large creature might make walking through it. She flashed her light toward the noise, then lowered it quickly. The brightness would only attract the beast to her.

"Right here." Thomas said.

Her heart leapt into her throat. She whirled around to find him just behind her. "Had to pee too," he said.

"You scared me!" She rushed back into the cabin, with Thomas coming behind and bolting the door. She dropped the flashlight and held the table, feeling weak and faint.

His eyes flashed with concern. He took her in his arms, holding her up, giving her strength. "Rose," he whispered. Tears sprang to her eyes at the tenderness in his voice. "Are you all right?"

"You called your dog." *I was terrified,* was left unsaid.

"Still looking for her."

"What if the alien heard you?" She sounded shrill.

"It's okay." Thomas smoothed her back. "We'll be okay."

She wanted to believe him. Already she felt better. His arms enclosed her like a warm, protective shield. For the moment she felt safe, though logically, there was no reason to believe his chances were any better than hers against a hostile invader.

Too soon, he let her go. She masked her disappointment as she leaned on the edge of the table. He was right, though. Any physical connection would only be a distraction. They needed to consider their situation.

Thomas got a blanket from the closet. "Take the bed, Rose."

"We're going to sleep?"

"Not me. You."

"Where will you be?"

"Right here." He sat on the recliner and drew the blanket over him. "I'll stay awake."

Rose walked to the bed and got under the covers. It felt lovely to lie down. She realized suddenly how exhausted she was, how desperately her body needed to sleep. She'd been in a shipwreck. They had hiked a long way in the afternoon. Of course she was exhausted. And if they had to fight a monster, wouldn't they stand a better chance of surviving after their bodies were replenished by rest?

She glanced at Thomas. "We can do shifts," she said. "Wake me up in a few hours."

He looked as if he would argue, but then he didn't. "If you want," was all he said.

"I do. It isn't fair to put it all on you. Because you're the man."

"Fine. And you know, I do have a plan," he said. "The plan is to get through tonight. In the morning, we can go to the dock on the other side of the island. There's a powerboat. Not a big one, but if we have to leave the island... it may be good enough."

"Okay. I feel better. We just have to make it through the night." She closed her eyes. Sleep must've come quickly after that.

Chapter Eighteen

KAILEY

WHEN THEY SENT me to solitary, I didn't think it would be that bad. I told myself I was used to being alone. I told myself it would only be one week, and that wasn't much time at all. I told myself I was strong enough to handle it. I was a fool, but I guess you know that already.

They let me outside for an hour each day. Outside meant a fenced-in enclosure small enough that if you put a pig in it, the animal rights people would complain. There wasn't room for a chair. It had a roof so I couldn't look up at the sky, but I had a clear view of the prison generator across the way. For most of the hour, I walked in tiny circles because the alternative was just standing there. Now and then, when I got dizzy from going round and round, I had to stop and lean against the fence.

For the great privilege of outdoor time in the chicken coop, I got strip-searched coming and going. I never could figure what I might've found inside my bare cell, or outside in the "yard," that could be used for any threatening purpose. But I soon realized the search had nothing to do with an expectation of finding something. They knew there would be nothing to find. It was just another way to make you suffer for whatever you did that landed you in solitary, as if living in a six by six concrete box wasn't hideous enough.

During my stay, I got to take two showers. They actually cuffed my wrists and ankles for the trip to the shower stall and back. They did release me long enough to undress and wash off quickly. But I think they would've shoved me in there fully clothed and chained, if they hadn't been worried the water would rust a good set of shackles.

The cell had a cot, a toilet, and a tiny sink. No books, Kindles, or anything else were allowed. I did stretches on the cot as there was no other place to do anything. I sat or lay in bed the entire time, except when I had to go to the bathroom. I dreaded taking a crap because the place would stink for the rest of the day.

I never thought I was claustrophobic, but lying there in a place without windows, surrounded by dirty gray walls so close it seemed like they were pressing in on me, like being in the *Star Wars* compactor… a sense of terror would overwhelm me. I'd sweat and then I'd have chills. My fingers got numb and my chest hurt. I felt like screaming. I didn't at first, but the last day I let loose and cried out till my throat was raw. No one ever came in to check on me. They probably looked in from the door and thought, no problem, just another inmate going stark raving mad.

It felt as if I was losing my mind. *Get a grip*, I kept saying. The Count of Monte Cristo survived twenty-one years of this. But then he was fictional, wasn't he?

At night it was worse. I lay awake for hours, with nothing to do but consider how my life could've turned out different. I tried to pinpoint the moment when it all went to hell. I think it might've calmed me a bit to figure it all out, to identify the place where I really messed up, to convince myself all would've been well if it weren't for that single mistake. Just one single goddamn mistake; surely I could be forgiven for that. But try as I might, I couldn't blot out the series of misguided choices that sent my life spiraling. The terrible, stupid, weak-minded decisions that culminated in the murder of a good man.

The problem lay with me and no one else. I obviously had a deeply flawed personality. I recognized that I was a coward. Afraid of confrontation, afraid of failure and rejection. Too frightened to take chances, to think for myself, to take a stand. As much as I told myself I didn't care about other people, I was deathly afraid of their opinions of me. Fear had destroyed any chance I'd had of a happy life, and fear made me wish for death as I lay trembling in this dark, dank hellhole.

I thought I would never amount to anything without conquering fear. And the little voice in the back of my head said, *you're in prison for the rest of your life; of course you'll never amount to anything.*

Chapter Nineteen

ROSE

ROSE WAS HAVING A NIGHTMARE. Somehow she knew it was a nightmare and yet she couldn't get it to stop. It came in dark flashes of disconnected imagery. A mirrored reflection of a man and a woman wearing ski masks. A gun in the man's hand. A small Asian man duct-taped to a chair, his mouth also taped, his eyes wide with terror. The sound of floorboards creaking as someone approached. The hand with the gun lifting up. *Blam.* The last sickening image to fill her mind was that of blood pooling under the old man's chair.

A dog barked. Rose thought it was part of her dream. But gradually her conscious mind woke and realized the bark was coming from somewhere outside. Somewhere in the distance.

She jerked awake. Her skin felt clammy. She looked around for her spear, which was where she'd left it, leaning against the wall near the table.

Thomas was no longer seated on the recliner. He was standing by the door, listening. He glanced back and saw she was awake. "It's Brandy," he said unnecessarily. He shot back the bolt and opened the door.

"You can't go out there!" She nearly screamed it.

Heavy darkness lingered outside. The wind had picked up. It sighed and moaned through the jungle.

"Brandy!" Thomas called out. He let out a loud, sharp whistle.

"The alien will hear you!" Rose sat up, the better to plead with him.

The dog barked again, still not very close.

"Brandy! C'mere, girl!" Thomas waited, searching for movement in the darkness outside. He drew back and shut the door.

"I'm sorry," Rose said. "There's nothing you can do for her." She wasn't really sorry. She was grateful he closed the door, and not really concerned about a random dog she'd never met.

Thomas grabbed his shoes and sat down to put them on.

Rose stared at him in disbelief. "What're you doing?"

"I'm going to find her."

"Are you crazy? She's just a dog."

"I guess you never had a dog."

She couldn't remember if she ever had one. She doubted it, because if she had, wouldn't she intuitively remember the love she'd felt for it? As it was, she understood people loved their pets, but she had no idea why.

"Don't open the door unless you hear my voice," he said, attaching the hatchet to his belt.

"You can't leave me! What if you don't come back?"

He hurried out with his spear in one hand, and a flashlight in the other, pulling the door shut behind him.

She crossed the room, picked up the roll of duct tape, and hurled it at the door. "Asshole!" she cried out. She opened the door and looked outside. The darkness had already swallowed him. There was no hope of getting him to return. She slammed the door shut and bolted it, before turning and throwing her back against it in frustration. She stared at the dark room and hugged herself.

Thomas had snuffed all the oil lamps while she was sleeping. She wondered if it was better to keep it dark. Maybe the alien, not seeing any light seeping out from the cracks around the door, might decide no one was home. *Who am I fooling?* Chances were the alien would sniff her out anyway, in which case she might as well light a lamp just to make herself feel better. And if it wasn't sniffing, it might be that it had extra-sensitive hearing, or infra-red vision, or even X-ray vision. It might have capabilities she couldn't possibly imagine.

She lit two lamps, one on the kitchen table, the other on the small table beside the recliner. She brought her spear and blanket with her and collapsed into the chair. She pulled the blanket over her and just sat there, staring at the flame of the lamp on the table. She tried not to think about what the creature might look like, or what it might be doing to Thomas and his dog at this very moment. But she couldn't think of anything else.

One thing was certain—she would not be going back to sleep. That was almost a relief, considering the nightmare she'd been having. She thought about the two figures reflected in the mirror. *The mirror.* Since she had been staring at a mirror, wouldn't that make the female figure herself? She'd worn a mask so it was hard to say. But the woman's size and shape did look right for Rose.

She wondered if the nightmare was based on one of her memories, or just some bizarre narrative her mind manufactured. Most dreams were the latter, weren't they? And yet something about it felt terribly real. Could she have imagined the frightened Asian man in such horrifying detail? What if it was a memory? That made her a criminal, perhaps even a murderer, though the man had held the gun. But she was with him, they were together. She couldn't imagine being part of such a thing.

For the first time, she wondered if she really wanted her memories back. Until now, she had simply assumed she'd been a good person, that her memories would be those of a full and happy life, surrounded by people who loved her. Why she had made such a naive assumption, she didn't know. From the store of information in her head, she knew there were all sorts of lives. Boring lives, sad lives, tortured lives, and lives that overran with evil. There were things it was better not to know. She could have a fresh start, with none of the baggage and the guilt that a normal human being carried throughout their lives. Maybe amnesia was a blessing in disguise.

After a while, she got up and tried pacing. She felt like a rat trapped in a cage, her fate subject to the whims of her captor. The alien hadn't put her inside there, but its very presence had forced her into a state of captivity. It had made her feel loneliness, terror, and hopelessness.

What felt like ages later, Thomas had still not returned. She had to do something, anything, to distract herself or she would lose her mind. Her gaze came to rest on Thomas's laptop. She stared at it for a moment before deciding to start it up.

The password prompt appeared. She typed Thomas's name, but that wasn't it. She tried his last name, with the same results. She grew excited at her next idea and entered "Brandy." That also was wrong. A message appeared notifying her she was locked out after the three failed password attempts.

She felt like flinging the machine out the door but held

herself back and merely shoved it aside. Still, her failure to access his files gave her another idea. Maybe he'd written his password down somewhere. She got up and began to search the place. At least it was a distraction from everything she didn't want to think about.

There was a small chest of drawers in the corner and she started with that. His boxers were jumbled in the top drawer, along with some toiletries. They were surprisingly colorful, with stripes and plaids and polka dots. One pair had images of a comic book superhero, the Black Panther. In contrast, his shorts and T-shirts, piled haphazardly in the other two drawers, were all plain colors: white and tan and gray. She wondered if she could take this as a metaphor for Thomas himself. A calm and unremarkable surface hiding a bizarre inner life. *But sometimes a boxer is just a boxer,* she thought.

There weren't any pencils or notepads in the drawers. It seemed that no one wrote anything on paper anymore.

She checked the drawers and cupboards in the kitchen. Mostly they held dishes and utensils. But her eyes lit up when she found slips of handwritten pages inside the third drawer. Only it turned out they were recipes: banana bread, chicken paprika, beef moussaka. Where did he expect to get chicken and beef? The man had no sense, as indicated by his running after a dog in the middle of the night with an alien in the vicinity.

She looked in the utility closet but found nothing resembling paper in there. She shut the closet door and leaned against it, her eyes scanning the room. Could it be in one of the books? It might take forever to find a scrap of paper in there. This search was futile. She no longer thought she had any chance of finding his password written down.

That was when she saw it. The box under the bed that he had said belonged to him. The box that attracted her curiosity when Thomas seemed to purposely refrain from telling her what was inside it.

She dragged it out from under the bed and opened it.

At first, she was disappointed. Some jeans, long-sleeved shirts, and a sweater were piled on top. Probably set aside in case colder weather ever came in. She was about to put the box back when she realized she was giving up too easily. What did she care if she made a mess searching the place? He had run out on her. She picked up the box and emptied its contents on the floor.

A wallet fell out from under the clothing. She opened it and stared at the driver's license in the windowed compartment. It wasn't the most flattering photo of Thomas, but it was definitely him. The problem was the name, which wasn't "Thomas Blackburn." The name printed on the license was "Alex Wright."

Rose slowly straightened. She couldn't take her eyes off it. *Why would he make up a name?*

She looked through the rest of the wallet and found two credit cards, also issued in the name of Alex Wright.

The door creaked. She whirled around, but no one was there. It was just the wind.

She looked back at the pile on the floor. It occurred to her that if Thomas came back, she didn't want him to know she'd found out his secret. At least, not until she was ready to confront him. She got down on her knees and gathered everything into the box, putting the wallet back in the bottom. She shoved the box under the bed.

She sat down to think about it. What reason could he have for lying about who he was? Maybe he was a wanted criminal. Someone well-known. At least, well-known to anyone who didn't have amnesia.

What if he's the man from my nightmare? For some reason, that hadn't occurred to her until now. A ski mask had covered his face. And the dream was too brief, too indistinct, for her to be able to picture his height or the color of his eyes. Hands could be recognizable, but she thought he was wearing gloves in the dream.

What if everything he told me was a lie? They were criminals, wanted by the law, hiding out here on this island when, of all things, an alien invasion occurred. Somehow she lost her memory and he didn't want to tell her about their past, maybe because it was just too disturbing.

A shout came from Thomas outside, his words indistinct. Rose froze up, as the hair lifted on the back of her neck. He cried out again, and this time she sprang up and grabbed her spear. She ran to the door, but hesitated in front of it, her breathing coming fast and hard. Her palm was sweaty as she clasped the door handle. She forced herself to turn it, to open the door, to peer outside at the shapes of trees and other things, swaying in the darkness. Leaves rustled, branches creaked, the generator went bang.

"Thomas?" Rose said weakly.

She strained to hear a reply, but he was silent now. Instead, she heard the snapping of branches and the crackling of leaves underfoot. The tromping of something heavy through the jungle.

"Thomas?" she whispered. When he didn't respond, she drew back, slammed the door, and bolted it. She threw her spear on the floor. *What good is it?* She didn't have the courage to use it. She was furious at herself for her weakness, and furious at Thomas for leaving her here alone.

WHOMP!

Something crashed against one of the shuttered windows, rattling the house. Rose screamed, looking around, desperate to figure out what to do. She blew out the lamp, retrieved her spear and backed up into a dark corner. An unnatural quiet settled over the place, more frightening than the noise that preceded it.

WHOMP! A blow against the window closest to Rose made her spasm. Her heart raced, her body shook uncontrollably. She pressed her hands over her ears.

WHOMP! The creature attacked the door. A piece of wood on the frame splintered. Another strike and it could give way. *What then?*

Rose forced herself to act. She got up, grabbed the bulky recliner, and dragged it in front of the door. She piled heavy things on top of it. Then she grabbed her spear, stepped back behind the chair, and waited with her shoulders tight, her lips trembling.

And she waited.

Once again it grew quiet. Even the wind seemed to stop. She looked around fearfully. Double-checked that her knife was firmly attached to the pole. She faced the door.

And she waited.

THOMP! THOMP! She jumped at the sound of noises overhead. *Was it on the roof now?* She looked up at the ceiling and realized the sound was rain. A sudden, heavy onslaught of rain.

An explosion of thunder came next. She wondered how she would hear the creature now.

A pounding began at the door. "It's me!" shouted Thomas. "Let me in!"

Relief flooded her. She hauled the chair aside and flung open the door. Thomas rushed in, slammed the door behind him, and stood there shivering, soaking wet from head to toe. Water dripped off him onto the floor. His spear and flashlight were gone.

"What happened?" Rose said.

"Need to dry off," said Thomas. He ducked into the washroom.

She locked the door and pushed the chair back against it. A moment later he emerged without clothes, a towel wrapped around his waist. He used another towel to dry himself.

"Did you see it?" Rose said. "I heard it... it tried to get in."

"Yeah, I saw it," he said, rubbing his arms with the towel. "I looked up from Brandy and there it was, twenty feet away. A huge dark shape. Hunched over. Its fingers clicking like they're nothing but bone."

"How did you get away?"

"I ran like hell," he said. "But shit, it's fast. Runs like an ape, all hands and feet." He dropped down on the bed. "It chased me to the beach. I knew I couldn't outrun it, so I stopped to face it. Tried to make myself big, you know, like they tell you to do against bears? I shouted and waved the spear." He rubbed the towel through his hair. "When it kept coming at me, I threw the spear at it."

"That stopped it?" she said.

"Hell no, it bounced right off. So I ran into the ocean and dove under. Swam for as long as I could without breathing. When I came up for air and looked back, the alien was gone. I kept swimming down shore, and then I got out."

"I can't believe you ran out on me! What if you were killed?"

"I had to try to save Brandy," he said.

"Where is she?"

"The alien killed her." He breathed out heavily.

"I'm sorry," she said. She *was* sorry, not so much about the dog, only for Thomas's sake. "But you shouldn't have gone. The creature came here, banging on everything. I thought it would break through the door." Her eyes filled with tears.

He went to her and wrapped his arms around her. It wasn't

fair. She wanted to be angry at him. She didn't think she should trust him. But when he held her like this, she couldn't stay angry at him. It was annoying as hell.

"I'm a coward," she said. "I heard your shouts. I wanted to help you, but... I just couldn't make myself."

"It isn't your fault. I don't blame you. You hardly know me," he said. "There's nothing you or I could've done anyway. The creature's too resilient."

"What're we going to do?" It was dreadful to think they were helpless to do anything besides waiting inside until the alien broke through the walls.

"Stay here until morning. Pray the creature sleeps by day. And head for the dock."

She looked at him and nodded. He was right, they would have to try to reach the dock. There was no other hope.

He looked down at the towel wrapped around his waist and seemed to recall himself. He took his clothing and went into the bathroom, where he changed behind the partly closed door.

Her head began to pound and she sat down on the bed. "Do you have any Tylenol?" she asked.

"I hope you don't have a fever," he said from behind the door.

"A wicked headache," she said. "It just started."

He came out fully dressed again and handed her a small bottle. He went to the kitchen and took out a glass.

"Do you usually get headaches?" he said.

"I don't know." It was incredibly frustrating not to know anything about herself. "Maybe. Maybe not. There's so much going on. Not just the alien. My memory, or lack thereof. Trying to sort through what's true and what's not..." She paused, hoping he would confide in her. *My real name is Alex*, he should say. She would forgive him for lying if he told her every-thing now.

"Sorting through what's true?" he said.

"Yes." She looked directly at him, challenging him to tell the truth.

He looked down and poured water for her.

"I had a dream," she said, hoping to provoke him.

He stopped short and looked up at her. "Oh?"

"Nightmare, really. It was awful. I seemed to be some sort of criminal." She stopped short of telling him a man was killed, and then waited, wondering if this would prompt him to admit their past.

His face went blank. He had to be hiding something, otherwise he ought to show some reaction to her revelation. "You think it was real?" he said.

"I don't know. It could've been. Maybe I'm haunted by a criminal past."

He let out a small laugh. "You're the last person in the world I'd picture as a criminal. Dreams are dreams. In mine, I can fly through the air without a plane, and survive a fifty-foot fall from the edge of a cliff." He brought the water over to her.

Rose swallowed two Tylenol with water and handed the glass back. She lay down and turned her face to the wall. If he wasn't willing to tell her the truth, she didn't want to talk to him.

Chapter Twenty

KAILEY

AFTER MY TIME IN SOLITARY, several weeks passed without any problems. I went back to my monotonous life of keeping to myself, exercising in the yard, and working at my boring job for most of the day. My one pleasure came at night, when I got to lie in bed and read until lights out.

For some reason Pall kept his distance. He didn't look at me, touch me, or even speak to me if he could avoid it. There were no more notes. I wanted to believe he'd lost all interest in me. But being a devious person myself, I was convinced it was just the opposite. *He's silently plotting his next move*, I thought. He was pretending not to notice me so that when he did act, it would take me completely by surprise and I wouldn't have any defense for it. In the meantime, it must've amused him no end to keep me guessing, to turn me into a quivering lump of anxiety as I worried about how to avoid the *something big* that was coming down any day now.

I tried never to be alone. I took showers at popular times. Ran in a loop around the basketball players outside. Ate at crowded tables. Went to bed after my roommates. Shit was less likely to happen when there were witnesses.

I was reading *Great Expectations* the night it happened. I'd been thinking how ironic the title was, both for Dickens' characters and for me. I was a person with zero expectations, let alone any great ones.

When the lights went out, I closed my Kindle and slid it under the bed. I shut my eyes, picturing Pip and Estella and Miss Havisham, thinking about what had happened to them so far, and what might happen to them in the future. I imagined myself as Estella, even though I didn't find her very likable. Maybe that made me relate to her all the more, I don't know. She also had a weird and difficult mother figure who appeared to be ruining her life. I enjoyed playing this game, immersing myself in the story world, which kept me from dwelling every night on my own insurmountable problems.

I was drifting off to sleep when Pall's hand clapped over my mouth. My eyes shot open and a scream arose in my throat, but he pulled tightly to muffle it.

"Get up," he hissed in my ear.

Helen, lying in the lower bunk across from mine, stared at the back of Pall, bent over me. I shifted my gaze to her, sending a silent appeal. She squeezed her eyes shut, making it clear there would be no help from that quarter. She followed the prisoner's mantra: *don't get involved.*

Pall drew his hideous face close to mine. "You say a word, you'll be back in solitary sooner than you can spit."

He drew back his hand. I wanted to scream and punch him, but the threat of solitary was too much for me. The wounds it caused were too recent, too deep. Often I woke in a cold sweat following a nightmare about being stuck forever inside that cell. And I knew, every time someone was sent to solitary, they made her stay longer than the time before. A second offense could get me three months. I'd be a babbling lunatic by the time I got out.

I rose slowly to follow him. He put his fingers to his lips, but I didn't need the reminder. I'd made my choice. I would submit silently to whatever the hell he wanted to do to me. Better than the torment of three months inside a concrete coffin.

He brought me to one of the shower stalls, where he turned me to face the wall and pulled down my prison pants. *At least I wouldn't have to look at him.* He paused to put on a condom, because if I got pregnant, we only had three male guards who could've done it, and he was one of them. *At least I wouldn't be having a baby in this godforsaken place.*

I stared at a crack in the tile and thought about Miss Havisham from *Great Expectations*, whose suffering was also caused by a man. Poor shriveled Miss Havisham in her yellowed wedding gown, with one foot in a torn and ragged silk stocking because she hadn't yet put on her shoe at the moment she was jilted. Poor abandoned Miss Havisham, who lived in a dreary house where all the clocks were stopped at twenty minutes to nine. Poor miserable Miss Havisham, who kept her unused wedding cake covered in cobwebs, in a room filled with spiders and beetles and mice. Bitter, angry Miss Havisham, driven to break a man's heart as hers had been broken. I squeezed my eyes shut thinking of her, while tears leaked out of them.

At least he was fast. He left me to wash off the stench of him before crawling back to my bed, making sure not to be seen by any other guard, because I would be the only one blamed for being up past curfew.

Chapter Twenty-One

ROSE

ROSE WOKE up coated in sweat. She felt as if she'd been haunted by nightmares, but she could only recall the briefest snippet of one of them. She was in prison, outdoors, wearing an orange jumpsuit, staring through a chain-link fence at the world beyond the prison. Mainly she remembered how she felt in that moment: as bleak and hopeless as the surrounding landscape.

When she sat up, pain shot through her head and it began to throb. She rose and filled her water glass, then swallowed two more Tylenol.

Thomas had fallen asleep on the chair, though she thought he'd said he would stay awake in case the alien returned. She looked around nervously at the door and windows, but nothing had changed. No aliens inside the cabin, at least.

Thomas opened his eyes. "Hey," he said. "You okay?"

"Yes… no. My head still hurts."

"Take some—"

She held up the bottle.

Thomas pulled himself up. "Sorry I fell asleep."

She shrugged. "Nothing happened."

He went to the counter and started a pot of coffee.

"I had another nightmare," she said. "I was in prison."

He glanced at her. "I've had those dreams before."

"What if it was real?" she said. "It felt real. What if I was behind bars before coming here?"

"If you were, how did you manage to join the research team?"

"I don't know. Maybe I was released. Maybe I escaped." She looked at him directly. "Maybe someone helped me escape."

He didn't return her look. "The other day, I dreamt I was on a steamship and it was sinking." He opened a cupboard and got out bread. "I couldn't leave the boat because I had to find my daughter to save her. It all seemed incredibly real. But I can tell you, since I don't have amnesia, that I've never been on a steamship, let alone a sinking one, and I don't have a daughter. Or a son, for that matter."

His point was made, and most likely he was right. Her head was pounding and she really didn't want to think about her nightmares anymore. "What are we going to do, Thomas?" she said. "How are we going to get out of here?"

"We'll eat breakfast. Then we'll go to the dock and leave in the boat."

"What about the alien?"

"It doesn't like the ocean. We'll walk on the shore."

"And jump in the water if it comes?"

"Yeah. You know how to swim?"

She couldn't remember ever swimming, but somehow she'd

made it back to this island from a sinking boat, without a life-jacket. "I think so," she said.

Thomas prepared plates with bread, butter, jam, cheese, and salami.

"Have you wondered why the alien came here on its own?" Rose said.

"They're probably going out all over the world, scouting places."

"Alone? In *Star Trek*, they never sent anyone out to scout by themselves. Two people at the minimum."

"I suppose *Star Trek* is the standard of alien exploration," Thomas said.

"It makes sense. If one is hurt, the other reports back."

"There's a lot to be said for the number two, I agree."

"Maybe it was shot down," she said. "Maybe we're up there fighting them."

"We probably are."

"I don't know. We haven't seen any other aircraft. Nothing at all. We haven't heard anything. The sky hasn't filled with toxic fallout. Admit it, there isn't a single sign of any sort of battle going on."

"True. But we're in the middle of nowhere. It may be quite a different story in New York City." He poured the coffee for them and brought the food to the table. "Hungry?"

She realized she was. The pain inside her head was lessening, and now she felt the hollow inside her stomach where food needed to be.

"Have any other ideas?" Thomas said.

She sat down, buttered her bread, and took a bite of it with a slice of cheese balanced on top. It tasted good. "What kind of cheese is this?"

"Cheddar," he said.

She spread strawberry jam on another section of bread

while she thought about the alien. "Maybe it's a deserter. Its own people shot it down when it tried to escape."

"Interesting idea," Thomas said.

"Greeks and Romans sometimes used slaves to row their ships. It's not uncommon for men to be forced into battle."

"The alien as slave labor... it's possible." He cut his bread in half and made a sandwich out of it, filled with jam, cheese and salami. "But even if it was forced into service... it doesn't necessarily make the creature friendlier to us."

"It's something to consider, that's all. Maybe the alien's only desire is escape." The first step in communication was understanding the motives of the other party. "Is there any instinct stronger than the yearning for freedom?" As soon as she said that, the prison image from her nightmare flashed in her mind, while a feeling of desolation swept through her.

She sipped from her coffee, then set down her cup. "I just realized something about myself."

Thomas raised his eyebrows.

"I'm not a coffee person."

"I'd make you tea, but we need to go."

She nodded. "I'll get some water." They got up and brought their plates to the basin.

"Shouldn't we bring supplies?" Rose said.

"There's stuff on the boat. I don't think we should slow ourselves down with a lot of weight."

Rose sat down to put on her sandals. Her gaze shifted to the box under the bed that held Thomas's wallet. *Or Alex's.*

"Don't you have a wallet? You might need that, if we make it," she said.

"Right," Thomas said.

He got out his backpack and began preparing it while Rose watched. His computer and power cord were the first things he put inside it. He added some crackers and a few water bottles, "to get us there." He went to the drawers and looked inside them, growing confused. Finally, he paused and looked around. "Not sure where I put it."

"Your wallet?" She decided not to tell him. She wasn't ready to reveal what she knew.

"Yeah," he said. He stood there thinking for a moment, then his eyes went to the box under the bed. He pulled it out and rummaged inside until finding his wallet at the bottom.

"Funny place for it," she said.

"Didn't think I'd be needing it for a while." He stuck it into his back pocket.

Rose took the one remaining spear. Thomas attached the hatchet to his belt again and threw on the backpack. "Ready?" he said.

Am I? she thought. *Am I ready to die?* Because that was what might happen out there. How would it be to die like this, not even knowing who she was? They say when death is near, your life flashes before your eyes. But what if you can't recall that life? Maybe her death would be less sorrowful. She would not regret separating from people she couldn't remember; she would not regret the loss of her most deeply felt experiences, because she had no idea what they were. Strangely, despite all of that, life was still sweet to her. It wasn't simply that she didn't want to die; she wanted desperately to live.

She nodded at Thomas and he opened the door. They both peered outside. The rain had gone as quickly as it came, but heavy cloud cover remained.

No monsters in sight.

Chapter Twenty-Two

KAILEY

REGARDING what Pall did to me, I've said enough for you to get what it was like. I don't want to dwell on it, other than to say, the State of California was really getting its money's worth when it came to my punishment.

I did consider telling someone about Pall. What stopped me every time I got close to talking, was the fear of solitary. If he knew I confided in anyone, he would have me framed before I had time to blink. He could've already hidden forbidden contraband somewhere in my room. Yolanda got a year in the hole when they found a crack pipe inside her mattress. *A year.* I couldn't bear it. I couldn't even bear the thought of it.

Six months passed, and then I got a urinary tract infection. As if things weren't challenging enough already, try seeing a doctor at Second Chance unless a hole opens up in your chest and your heart falls out. I waited two hours to get on the list to see a doctor, and they gave me an appointment for a week later. The pain when I peed was excruciating, but that was my problem. I'd have to wait for the diagnosis before I could get medication.

I curled up in my bed feeling miserable that night. Along with everything else, I was terrified Pall might show up. I hadn't seen him in three weeks. Like a bad penny—an evil, twisted, malevolent penny—he always came back. He just had to wait for the right opportunity, like when the other guards were taking naps or watching TV.

Lights had been out for a few hours, and I was lying there feeling like I had to pee even though I'd gone twenty minutes earlier. I didn't want to go again because whenever I did, it felt like broken bits of glass flowing through me. While I was trying to decide if I could bear it, Pall showed up. He threw me a nod that meant, *get up and come with me.* I cringed and turned toward the wall, clutching the blanket around me.

He leaned down and shook my shoulder. "C'mon."

"Can't," I said. "I got a UTI. A bladder infection." He probably didn't know what a UTI was.

"Fuck I care," he said. "Get up."

I shook my head and didn't turn around. I couldn't bear it, it hurt so goddamn much already.

He grabbed my arm and started to pull me. "Bitch, you know what happens if you cross me."

I saw Bridget peering over from the top bunk. She drew back when she saw me look at her. Hear no evil, see no evil.

"No!" I cried out. I wasn't thinking straight. I should've told him he would catch it from me. That might've worked.

He let go and hissed into my ear, "You're gonna be sorry."

Chapter Twenty-Three

ROSE

"WE SHOULD MOVE QUICKLY," Thomas said.

Rose, resisting the impulse to tell him that much was obvious, nodded and followed him out. They speed-walked toward the beach, while she checked frequently behind them. Every puff of air, every shifting of shadows under the trees, put her on edge. Branches rustled as if something large was moving through them.

"Faster, if you can," Thomas said.

They picked up the pace and reached the shore a few minutes later. Rose paused, eyeing the beach. Something didn't feel right about it.

Thomas glanced at her. "What is it?"

"Isn't this where I washed up?"

"Yeah," Thomas said, uninterested. "We need to hurry."

"But there's nothing here now."

"What do you mean?"

"The stuff scattered around from the shipwreck."

Thomas stared up and down the beach. It was pristine. "The tide must've taken it out," he said.

"Even the piece of hull?"

"I guess. Unless our alien wanted it for his nest."

The reminder of the alien was enough to keep her from dawdling. Why was she thinking about the shipwreck anyway? That was over; her colleagues' lives must've been claimed by the sea. She felt sorry for them in an abstract way, as if they were people she read about in the newspaper. Without remembering them, it was impossible to have stronger feelings about their loss.

Hurrying up beside Thomas, she said, "When we get to the boat, where will we go?"

"We'll head to Hawaii. It's the closest place."

"Will we have enough gas?"

"There should be extra stored in the building. We can make it. If the weather holds out."

Rose looked at the jungle. "I suppose there are worse ways to die than being stranded in the Pacific."

They came to a section of rock they needed to climb. Thomas paused to give Rose a hand up. Her sandals didn't grip well, and she needed to slow down to avoid slipping.

"I wish I didn't feel this way," she said. "Afraid to stay here, and afraid to go back."

"Unlike before, I want to go back," Thomas said. "I want to know what's happening. Now I know there's no place on earth that's immune from invasion."

"It isn't only that. I'm afraid of what might be waiting for me. Afraid of finding out who I am, I suppose."

"We're all afraid of finding out who we really are."

"Is that supposed to be philosophical?" she said.

He shrugged.

"Who are you, Thomas Blackburn?" She pictured his wallet, with another man's name under his photograph.

He paused and looked at her. "Time will tell, I guess."

"Why are you here alone?" she said. "You never really answered that."

"Needed time to think over my life."

"That sounds like a cliché," she said. "Are you running away from something?" *Did you kill a man?* she wanted to say. *Did you come here to hide from the law?*

Thomas slipped on the rock. He fell hard and banged his knee. "Shit!" he said.

She kneeled beside him. "Are you okay?"

He grimaced. "I'll be fine. Need to pay better attention."

She gave him a hand up. He took a careful step and his leg buckled. Rose caught hold of his arm.

"You can lean on me," she said.

They moved at a slower pace. After a few minutes, they climbed down from the rocks and continued on sand. Thomas limped slightly but was able to increase his speed before long.

They walked in silence for some time, until Thomas stopped and pointed at something in the distance.

"The dock is there," he said. "Not much farther." They sped up.

Thomas led the way to a mid-sized, dilapidated building with a crooked sign: "U.S. Department of Fish & Wildlife." They hurried past, toward a wooden plank going down to the dock.

There were no boats tied up.

Rose threw an anxious look at Thomas. "Where is it?!"

He wore a shocked expression. "I don't know." His throat sounded dry. "It should be here. You guys said you'd leave the powerboat. You were taking the sailboat." He laid down the spear, dropped his pack on the ground, and ran down the plank. Rose followed him.

He checked the edge of the dock for a tie line. Part of the rope was still there. When he held it up, they saw it was frayed at the end.

"The storm must've caused this." He scanned the horizon. "The boat must've drifted out."

Rose felt panic welling inside her. "Maybe it drifted back somewhere else on the island." Her eyes searched the horizon. "But we need it *now*. We need it *here*."

Thomas straightened. "C'mon." He bounded up the plank, grabbed the spear and backpack, and went into the building. Rose went after him.

Inside, Thomas began checking the rooms while Rose looked around the main area. There was a basic kitchen and dining section, with a long wooden table and rickety chairs. Beside this was a large gathering area, with a high ceiling, a stone fireplace, a moth-eaten couch and worn armchairs.

Rose went to the refrigerator and opened it. It wasn't running and felt warm inside. The shelves were empty save for something covered in fungus at the back. She checked the cupboards next. Nothing but dust and crumbs.

Thomas came up behind her. "You guys didn't leave anything."

It sounded like an accusation. *Are you responsible for things you don't remember doing?* She didn't think she was the sort of person to withhold food from the one other person on the island. Could the knock on her head have changed something essential about who she was? She couldn't relate to this woman who had sailed off on a boat without any thought given to the man left behind.

Thomas stepped into a storage area behind the kitchen. Rose glanced into one of the bedrooms. There were two bunks with bare mattresses, and an empty dresser with the drawers pulled open. Was this where she'd lived? It looked depressing.

"Fuckers," said Thomas. "They took the gas cans too. No fuel for the generator."

At least he'd switched pronouns from "you" to "they." He was starting to view her differently than the woman she was before amnesia. She watched as he threw himself into a chair.

"They?" she said.

"I think it was Dave. That guy was a prick."

"I hope I wasn't the sort of person who would do this to you." She sat across from him. "But maybe we had our reasons." *Maybe we found out something disturbing about you. Maybe we left you behind on purpose, because we discovered you weren't who you said you were.*

He looked up sharply. "What do you mean?"

Did she really want to confront him now? "Nothing," she said. She glanced around. "So this is it. We aren't going anywhere."

"Not unless you're a long-distance swimmer."

"Do you know how to build a boat?" she said.

"Nailing those shutters closed was the limit of my carpentry skills. How about you?"

Strangely, when she thought about it, she actually could picture the steps for building a boat. "We might be able to figure it out," she said. "The problem is finding the right tools and materials." Her gaze shifted to the refrigerator. "How much food do we have?"

"Maybe a month's worth of the stuff I brought with me," he said. "I've got fishing rods, though. There's coconuts and some other edible plants. We have water from a creek that runs down from the hills. Food and water aren't the issue."

Rose glanced at the windows and shivered. "I suppose we'll have to deal with the creature."

"How do you propose?"

"We can try and trap it."

"Sure," he said. "Let's make a pit with knives sticking up at the bottom. Cover it with palm fronds. Entice the alien there with the smell of fish."

"You're being ridiculous again."

"Well what's your plan?"

"I don't have one." She stood up. "But maybe we could start by being honest with each other, *Alex.*"

Thomas stared at her and blinked.

She got up and went to the window, where she stared out at the tangle of trees bordering the sand. *Where is it now?* she thought.

Chapter Twenty-Four

KAILEY

I SEARCHED my room every day for a week without finding anything. It was driving me crazy, wondering if the contraband was already there but I was missing it. This was the way Pall fucked with your mind. He never did anything too fast, because that would take all the fun out of it. Some people loved to create a happy anticipation for a joyful event. Pall was the opposite. He thrived on the dread you felt as you waited for the terrible shit you knew was coming your way.

The next day, one of the inmates I was a little bit friendly with rushed up to me and said she overheard two of the guards saying they were going to "inspect" my room. I thanked her and walked as fast as I could back there; any faster and I would've been stopped for running.

The place was empty when I got back, so I figured they must not have come yet. If they'd already arrived and done their search, they would've found something and they'd be waiting for me. The only reason to search my room at all would be if Pall had tipped them off that there was something to find. And where to find it.

I started a frenzied hunt through my things, praying he'd made it easy to be sure the guards found it. I tried inside my pillow case, under the bed, in my drawer... there wasn't anything I hadn't put there myself. I wracked my brain for other places to look. That's when I remembered the Kindle. I hadn't thought to check under its cover until now.

I heard the voices of the guards approaching and dove for the Kindle, opening it up, holding it upside down. A metal razor fell out. I snatched the razor up and looked frantically for some place to hide it. It couldn't be anywhere on me; they'd be sure to search me. *Shit.* I could hear their footsteps now.

The bottle of shampoo on the table caught my eye. It was my only chance. I unscrewed the cap and pushed the razor down inside the fluid. The guards were almost here. I fumbled with the cap, screwing it on as fast as my fingers would move.

"Turn around!" This came from Edie—or *Beastie* as we called her behind her back.

I quietly set down the bottle and slowly swiveled around. Sly-eyed, puffy-faced Beastie and vacant Cerise who couldn't make a decision if her life depended on it, lurked behind me.

"Need you to stand over here," Beastie said.

I followed her gesture to a spot just outside of the cube. Beastie and Cerise began to search the place.

"What're you doing?" I said.

"What's it look like?" Beastie shook my pillow out of its case but didn't bother to look inside. They spent a few minutes making a pretense of not knowing where the razor was, before finally taking out my Kindle and opening it up.

I felt like laughing at the surprised look on Beastie's face when she didn't find what she was looking for, but I managed to keep a straight face as she turned her suspicious gaze on me.

Cerise had paused to watch us. "Keep looking!" Beastie barked. They tore the place apart looking for the razor, while I stood there with my arms wrapped around me, trying to stifle my trembling. If they found the razor, there was no question I was headed to solitary for at least three months.

Finally, Beastie called off the search. I held my breath until they left the area. I still had the razor. They hadn't thought to open the bottle and pour the shampoo out.

Chapter Twenty-Five

ROSE

THOMAS JOINED her at the window. "Does it really matter who I am at this point?" he said.

"Yes, it matters. It's the difference between the truth and a lie. How do I know you haven't lied about other things?"

"Fair enough. My name is Alex Wright. Mean anything to you?"

"No. Nothing."

"I'm the founder of a company called Vytal Tech. V-Y-T-A-L."

"I don't see what that has to do with anything."

"My company's very successful," he said. "I'm worth a lot. I didn't want to be recognized when I came here. I'm sick of people fawning over me. I never know if they're genuine or just working me for something. Most often it turns out to be the latter."

"You came here to get away from them?"

"That's right. To be alone, and if I saw anyone, I would tell them a made-up name so they would treat me like a human being, instead of a cash machine."

"None of us knew who you really were?"

"Yeah. I'm sorry I lied to you," he said.

Rose still had no idea whether to believe him or not. She *wanted* to believe him. He was standing next to her and their shoulders were touching. She pictured him wrapping his arm around her and holding her closer.

"Do you want to know how my wife died?" he said.

She did, very much, but she pretended to be uninterested. She wasn't ready to forgive him for deceiving her. "If you want to tell me," she said.

"I was sitting right next to her when the bullet came. One bullet. That's all it took."

"Who shot her?" *Please don't tell me you did.*

"It was one of those random shootings you hear about all the time. A crazy man at a shopping mall. We were in the food court. He injured twenty-three people. Killed five, including himself."

Rose pressed closer to him, not realizing she was doing it at first.

"I heard the shots, but then I froze," he said. "I should've grabbed her and pushed her down. Shielded her with my own body. But no, I just sat there and let her die."

She looked at his face, but there weren't any tears. More like a stoic acceptance. "Is that why you needed time alone, here on this island?"

He nodded.

They stood together staring out the window. Rose leaned her head against his shoulder.

After a moment, he raised his hand and smoothed her hair.

He kissed her forehead lightly. A deep sense of contentment surged through her, followed by a stabbing regret at their situation, being stalked by a beast, when all she wanted was for Thomas to hold her and kiss her and whisper tender words in her ear.

"We should go back to the cabin," he said softly. "At least there, we've got food and supplies. We can search for the boat later."

"Yes. There's nothing for us here," Rose said. She felt a chill as Thomas stepped away from her to put on his backpack. They paused at the door, checking for any sign of the alien, seeing nothing. Then they went out.

Thomas stopped a short distance from the building. "I left the spear back there. You mind getting it? That'll give me a chance to take a leak."

"Sure," Rose said.

"It's against the wall near the couch."

She hurried back up the stairs into the building. The spear was where he'd described. She grabbed it and turned back toward the door.

The sickening cry of the alien arose from outside. Rose's breath caught in her throat as she froze in place, her body tingling with fear.

"Stay back!" Thomas called out.

There were sounds of a struggle. He needed her help, she had the spear. But it felt as if her feet had been nailed to the floor. The alien wailed again.

Rose took slow breaths, trying to concentrate on calming herself enough to move and take action. An eerie silence settled over the place, more frightening than the noises that came before. Her hands went clammy with sweat. What if she looked out the door to find the alien waiting for her? *What if Thomas is already dead?*

She couldn't allow such thoughts to poison her mind. She might still be able to save him, but not if she continued to cower inside the building. In any case, she couldn't remain in there forever.

She managed to step forward, forcing herself closer to the door, trying to remain concealed in case the creature was searching for her. Seconds later she glimpsed the outside. A huge dark form was carrying Thomas, apparently unconscious, on its back. The alien was bent over like a giant ape, its skin glistening like that of a lizard.

They disappeared into the jungle.

A sense of dread filled her. She pulled back into the room, shaking her head wildly. "No... no!" She sank down on her heels. "Don't leave me, Thomas," she whimpered. *"Don't leave me."* She buried her face in her hands.

She wasn't sure how long she remained like that, her mind crippled by fear. Gradually she got control of herself, forced her hands from her face, and rose up.

Rose took a shaky step outside and scanned the horizon, but there was no Thomas, and no alien, to be seen. She struggled to swallow the growing despair inside her.

Chapter Twenty-Six

KAILEY

I KNEW Pall would wait several weeks and try again. At first I thought he would choose a better hiding place for whatever contraband he picked the next time. Then he would come and find it himself, instead of sending proxies.

But on second thought, I decided he would choose a different method. Pall wasn't one to repeat himself. He loved to keep his victims guessing. If he wasn't such a sadist, I probably would've started to admire him. He had a special talent for torture and manipulation. No wonder he liked working as a prison guard.

I thought he might bribe some of the tougher inmates to beat me up. If they planned it well, they'd jump me when no one else was around. They'd hurt me fast, and then disappear. Injured and helpless on the ground, I wouldn't be able to run away. I would be the only one found, the only one who had obviously been in a fight. It wouldn't matter that I clearly lost the fight, I would be punished. Yeah, getting the crap kicked out of you in prison is a punishable offense. The guards would ask you for names, but of course you couldn't tell them, or you might get killed the next time. In the end, the authorities figured either you were part of the fight and should be punished for it, or you were a victim who needed protection. Either case landed you in solitary. You'd be safe there, where no one could get to you. That was the reasoning.

My life had been transformed by a monster. Before Pall came, I could tolerate prison. But now I was constantly on edge. Everywhere I went, my eyes darted from side to side, looking for enemies, searching for anything that might get me in trouble. At night I barely slept, thinking of all the things that could happen in the dark. I dreaded the possibility—no, likelihood—of getting sent back to solitary. I was losing weight and feeling weaker by the day.

The irony was, Pall himself had given me a possible way out. I'd been thinking about it every night since my room was searched, until the chance literally fell into my hands. I was in the shower, pouring out shampoo, and the razor flowed out of the bottle on its own. I rinsed it off and stared down at my wrists while the water ran over me.

Can I do it? I'd berated myself for my cowardice. Always too frightened to make the tough choices. Always letting fear rule my life.

Here was my chance to prove my courage. I had the means to determine my own fate. It was my decision. I could end this hell now if I wanted to. No longer would I have to live under anyone else's control. The power to choose death lay with me.

My death would hurt no one, least of all my mother. She'd washed her hands of me long ago. The few friends I had in high school had never been in touch. Noah… he'd showed how much he cared for me when he delivered me up to the DA.

What had I done on this earth, besides taking up space and exploiting resources that could've been put to better use? The State of California could use the money they spent on me to feed some homeless people instead.

I stared at my wrists. How long would it take for the blood to drain out of me? Usually people sat in warm water in a bathtub to help speed things along. I could make the shower water hotter, but it wouldn't be the same. My blood gathering around the slow drain would be spotted by someone long before I was dead.

There was another way. It would be harder to do, but its effects would be quick. I lifted the razor to my neck and prepared to slash through it.

Chapter Twenty-Seven

ROSE

ROSE BROUGHT the spear to the clearing by the building and tried hurling it. It went no more than ten feet, wobbled, and dropped to the ground. *Pathetic.* Spear-throwing was clearly out of the question; she might just as well hand the alien her weapon. Her only hope would be to draw near enough to thrust it into the beast. She hoped it didn't have skin like armor.

Rose fetched the spear and stared at the place where the alien, carrying Thomas, had disappeared under the trees. It seemed she had two options: to chase after them or pray for Thomas to manage his own escape. But she recognized the second choice as a hopeless one. She believed neither in the power of prayer, nor in Thomas's ability to overcome the much larger creature without the advantage of surprise. She thought about returning to the cabin and working out a plan to sneak into the alien's enclave and steal Thomas back. But how long would the creature keep Thomas alive?

With every second she delayed, Thomas could be inching closer to death. She had to go after him now. Despite the slippery feel of the spear inside her damp palm, she forced herself forward, one uncertain step at a time, toward the shrouded jungle. Thomas's backpack lay ahead on the ground where it must've fallen off him, marking the entrance to the rough path they had taken. Apparently even the alien found it too taxing to trample through the vines and bushes thickly clustered between the trees. As Rose started on the path, she listened closely in case Thomas called out for her. But the only sounds came from twigs crunching under her feet, and branches slapping against her body, despite her every effort to approach in silence.

She stopped to listen again, and to peer in all directions in case they'd left the trail. She couldn't tell if the sound she heard was breathing, or the groan of tree trunks swaying in the breeze. Frightened but determined, she pressed onward.

The alien wailed. It began as a long, thin whine that stretched into dissonance. Rose dropped her spear and clapped her hands over her ears. She remained rooted in place, shivering, until the last echo dissipated.

She struggled to settle herself with slow, steady breaths, but the air had become stifling. A heavy, sickening scent like tar filled her nose and made her gag. *Is it the stench of the alien?* She breathed in through her mouth to keep from smelling it.

She snatched up her spear and continued forward, driving herself onward. She glimpsed movement in the distance, a shadowy form swaying. She kept going, treading lightly, struggling not to make a noise, with her weapon braced tightly in front of her.

Growing closer, she left the path, drawing behind bushes,

creeping nearer. Abruptly, the alien came into clear view, no more than twenty feet ahead of her.

Rose suppressed a gasp.

The beast was hideous. Peeling skin the color of dried blood. Its enormous body, twice as large as the biggest apes, hunched over, with tiny eyes in its bulbous head. A dripping mouth filled with fangs.

Thomas lay on the ground beside it, unconscious or dead.

While Rose watched, the creature slowly raised its eyes to her. Staring. Its bone fingers clicking furiously.

Something came over her then. A certainty that she could never defeat it. The beast was so much larger and stronger than her, there was no point in even trying. But it was more than that. Her mind filled with the collective history of battles waged, lives lost, all to no real purpose. Killing wasn't the answer. Killing had never been the answer.

Clutching her spear with a shaking hand, she slowly advanced, one foot and then the next, until she halved the distance between them.

The alien watched her with eerie stillness, ready to pounce on her if it chose.

Rose held the spear in front of her with both hands and dropped down onto her knees. She lay the weapon on the ground and lowered her head. She understood this would most likely be the moment of her death, and if so, it would be a violent and bloody passing.

"I wish you no harm," she said, without any idea if the creature could hear or comprehend her words. She had no way of knowing if the gestures of surrender and friendship were the same between their vastly different cultures. She waited with her head bowed for a sign from the alien, but there was only silence.

At last Rose looked up to find the alien gone. She whirled

her head sharply in case it had crept behind her, but it wasn't there either. She stood and scanned every direction without catching any sign of the creature.

Thomas opened his eyes and saw Rose. He sat up, suddenly wary, looking forward and backward as Rose had. "Where is it?" he whispered.

"I don't know, it went away after I spoke to it." She knelt at Thomas's side and they hugged each other fiercely. "Are you all right?"

He nodded. "You followed us?"

She told him everything that had happened since the alien carried him away.

"You were so brave. Coming here. Risking everything. Thank you." He looked at her and smoothed the hair from her brow, his own face suffused with emotion.

"I wasn't brave, I was terrified," she said. "But I thought this was our only chance. They're bigger than we are, and they must be smarter too, because they came all this way. If they want to destroy us, they will." She shivered. "I didn't want to look at it or hear its awful voice."

"You showed empathy," he said.

"I didn't want to kill it, though I might've tried if that was the only way to save you," she said. "It seemed wrong to attack it without even attempting to communicate."

"You were smart, Rose. Smart and kind."

"I'm not sure. The alien could've killed us both."

"You did everything right," Thomas said. "You found the courage to come here and rescue me."

She looked around nervously. "I don't know if it's over. It might still return. It might try to hurt us again."

Thomas nodded. "We should go back to the cabin. We'll have time to consider everything there."

Chapter Twenty-Eight

KAILEY

OF COURSE, you know I didn't slit my throat or I wouldn't be here telling you my story.

I came very close. I had the razor pressed so hard against my skin, some blood oozed out and got on my fingers.

I believe what stopped me was picturing Pall's triumph. I didn't think he'd care that he no longer had me to rape. There were plenty of other inmates around for him to target. His true pleasure came in fucking with your mind, as well as your body. Pushing me to suicide would be the ultimate fuck job. He'd probably go back home and have a blue ribbon made up for himself.

I could not let him win. I lowered my hand, rinsed off the blood, and put the razor back inside the shampoo bottle. When I wrapped the towel around my hair, I made sure to cover the tiny nick in my neck. After that I did the thing that had frightened me more than the idea of killing myself.

There was one guard, Ashley, who was nicer than the rest. She would never be my best friend, but you could see the sympathy in her face when certain things happened that weren't fair. You could reason with her in a way that didn't work with any of the other guards. She was my only chance. I went to her and told her exactly what Pall had been doing to me. I gave her the shampoo bottle with the razor still inside.

She looked worried, which made me fear she would be too afraid, too ineffectual, to help me. That Pall had too much influence and would be believed over her. That it was all just too much trouble, and after all, I was a murderer serving a life sentence, so what good would it do to help me anyway? She told me not to say anything to anyone else, muttered a few more words I couldn't hear, and went away.

The next day she returned and took me to the warden's office. The warden's name was Mrs. Fleischer. I don't know why, but I looked it up one day and found out it meant "butcher" in German. I wondered if her grandfather had run a concentration camp, as it seemed like a fitting name for that. Prison was similar in some ways. It was hard to believe some people actually chose to oversee a prison or a concentration camp. I didn't put much faith in Mrs. Fleischer being a good person who might sympathize with me.

She was at her desk, looking at her computer, when I was ushered in. For some reason the razor blade was also on her desk, as if Mrs. Fleischer wanted to show me the evidence. It made me think of the courtroom during my trial. "Your honor, I would like to submit Exhibit A," one of the lawyers would say.

The warden was about fifty, with straight gray hair and a stern expression. She wore a business suit with a tie, and reading glasses balanced at the tip of her nose. After a pause, she glanced up and gestured for me to sit. I took the chair in front of the desk and kept my gaze lowered.

"Tell me what happened in your own words," she said.

I had the warden's ear, which might never happen again. Now was not the time to hold back, whatever might come of it. I probably told her much more than I should have, and much more than she wanted to hear. But she kept her expression steady through every revolting detail of what he did to me in the shower each time.

When I finished she said, "How long has this been going on?"

"Nearly a year," I said.

"You should've come to me sooner," she said.

I was afraid, I thought. *Afraid of you. Afraid of Beastie and the other guards. Afraid of the inmates. Afraid of Pall. Afraid of the deep, bitter hole inside myself that I would have to confront again if you sent me to solitary.*

The Warden scrutinized me. "What made you act this time?"

I kept silent and shrugged. The truth was, I didn't have a clear answer to that. All I knew was I'd had the chance to pick death, and instead I chose life.

Chapter Twenty-Nine

ROSE

SHE BECAME MORE SETTLED once she and Thomas were back inside the cabin, though there was much she didn't understand regarding her encounter with the alien. Why did the creature simply leave? If it understood her offering and wanted to communicate, why not make a reciprocal gesture? For all she knew, it might've left them alone for an unrelated reason. It needed to drink water or relieve itself. An urgent message had come in from the mother ship, and the alien had to return to its own vessel to respond. The creature might come back any minute now. *It might still be hungry.*

Yet, maybe because they'd survived the night inside the cabin, the place gave her the illusion of safety. Especially when Thomas was there with her.

He looked at her with concern, probably due to her silence

and the uncertainty that must've shown in her face. He touched her shoulder. "Are you all right?"

That was all it took to release the fear, tension, and fatigue that had been building up inside her. She started to cry in heavy, jagged gulps. He wrapped his arms around her and muttered something soothing, while she wet his shirt with her tears.

She calmed down after a few minutes and just remained still in his arms, not wanting him to let go of her. When she finally did look up, it was to raise her hands around his neck and draw his lips to hers. He gave her a real kiss this time, long and tender and filled with desire. When it ended she took his hand to bring him to the bed.

He shook his head. "No, Rose," he said gently.

"Why not?" she said. She didn't understand why he still hesitated.

"It's not a good time," he said.

"Because of your wife?"

He paused briefly before saying, "That's right."

Even though it was a valid reason, his rejection stung. If he wasn't over his wife's death, how had he managed to kiss Rose like that? As usual, what he did and what he said didn't match up.

He turned from her, went to the closet, and took out a fishing rod. "I'm going to catch dinner," he said.

"The alien is out there." She wondered how he could be so matter-of-fact. They still understood nothing about the alien's intentions. "It might decide to go after you again."

"I'll be at the water. I can swim if I need to." He grabbed a tackle box and hurried out of the cabin.

Too hurt and angry to call him back, she threw herself down on the bed. *Why is he so stubborn?* She lay down on her back and stared at the ceiling. But it wasn't long before exhaustion overtook her and she fell asleep.

It wasn't a restful sleep. Images kept appearing inside her head. First it was the beach where she'd washed up. She was sitting beside Thomas, looking around. Something didn't feel right, but she didn't know what. Things went dark, and then she was running out of the cabin, with Thomas behind her. She recognized this as the memory from when the alien ship hurtled through the sky. But she and Thomas were staring up at nothing at all. The sky was empty, and the noise they'd heard when the spaceship plummeted and crashed was gone.

The image inside her head shifted. She was at the crash site in the jungle, kneeling on the ground, making strange movements with her arms and legs. As if she was climbing, and yet there was nothing to climb. *The alien craft wasn't there.* It was an empty clearing with no smoke, no ship, no nothing. Blackness filled her mind again, and then she was standing next to Thomas. He was pointing at the place where they'd found the alien cocoon. But nothing was there besides the tangle of low-growing plants.

Her dream faded and re-formed. She was in the jungle where she'd found Thomas. He lay unconscious on the ground as before, but now there was no menacing creature hovering near him. She could swear she was staring at the spot where she'd confronted the alien, but the place was empty.

Rose woke abruptly and looked around, feeling alert, no longer drowsy. She was still alone in the cabin. Checking the clock, she found she'd only been dozing for ten minutes. As she got up, a painful throbbing arose in her head. She swallowed more Tylenol.

Such a bizarre sequence of dreams. As if her subconscious wanted to strip the alien out of existence.

She sat at the kitchen table, thinking. Everything had been

strange since coming here. Even Thomas, she had to admit. She wanted him to be the one real thing, the person she could count on and trust. *But he lied to her.* How could she trust a man who didn't tell her the truth about himself? She wondered if there was more she ought to know. She had searched the inside of the cabin. What about the outside? She remembered seeing a small storage locker in the back when Thomas had gone around the house nailing the shutters in place.

Rose went out and walked around the building to check the box. When she discovered the latch was secured with a padlock, suspicion filled her regarding what might be hidden inside. Maybe he had locked it to keep the contents safe from the alien, but she thought she recalled seeing the padlock there earlier. Which could only mean Thomas locked it to keep *Rose* from seeing what was kept there.

She straightened and listened for sounds of Thomas returning, but a still silence hung over the place. Returning to the front of the cabin, she squinted toward the water and saw no sign of him. Inside the building, she searched the drawers and cabinets for a key. Since she was already pretty familiar with the contents of everything, it didn't take long before she turned up emptyhanded. Chances were good Thomas kept the key with him.

Determined to find out what was inside the box, she grabbed the hammer and returned outside. It actually felt good to let her frustrations pour out as she whacked at the latch. For five minutes, she pounded away, but it held fast. She lowered the hammer and leaned against the wall, praying the noise hadn't reached Thomas, wherever he was. After catching her breath, she raised the hammer one more time and smashed it down as hard as she could.

The latch broke off and Rose tossed the hammer aside in triumph. She raised the lid.

Two items only lay inside. The first was a comm box like the one Thomas had described to her. Lights flashed on its display. Its cord led into the house through a small hole, meaning it was plugged in and powered by the generator. Examining it more closely, she could see that one of the lights indicated a signal was being received. Thomas did have working communications here. *Another lie.*

She shifted her gaze to the other item, a small pistol resting beside the box. *The worst of all the lies.* Thomas had told her he didn't have a gun. When they were most in need of protection, he'd lied and told her how un-American he was for not owning a firearm. And yet here it was.

A nervous shiver swept through her. His lies and concealment were worse than she could've imagined. To think she'd been falling in love with the man. She looked around again for any sign of him. He could easily have heard the banging and might walk around the corner any second now.

She ran back into the cabin, grabbed the backpack he'd been using, and threw water bottles, a box of crackers, and a can of almonds into it. She wracked her brain to think of anything else she might need. *The flashlight. A blanket.* Most likely she was forgetting something essential but she had no time.

She ran out, then hesitated. *There's one more thing.* She returned to the open box and picked up the gun gingerly. It was weird, but as she had already experienced with some other items, she seemed to have knowledge of how a gun worked. This one didn't have a magazine attached, which must mean it was unloaded, but she knew there could still be a bullet left in the chamber. If she peered straight into it, she ought to be able to find out, but she didn't relish accidentally blasting herself in the face. She was tempted to shoot at the sky just to get rid of any bullet that might be there, but two things stopped her. One was that the sound would certainly bring Thomas to the cabin instantly. The other reason was... if things became desperate... if Thomas was the villain he now appeared to be... she might need some defense.

Slipping the gun into a pocket in the backpack, she fervently hoped her movement wouldn't trigger it. She ignored the raindrops that began falling fast and hard as she set out toward the jungle.

Chapter Thirty

KAILEY

PALL WAS FIRED IMMEDIATELY and rape charges were filed. I didn't look forward to testifying against him, but I would do my best to get him convicted. It gave me a bit of sadistic pleasure to imagine his reception behind bars, when the inmates found out he used to be a guard. But the chances of conviction weren't high, it being my word against his. I didn't have any evidence like a soiled red dress, ha, ha. Not even a soiled orange jumpsuit, because you don't exactly have a place to stash dirty clothes or anything. I didn't expect my word to count for much at the trial, considering I'm a convicted killer. But at least I would be safe from him now.

After word got around that I'd turned him in, I got more respect. I was sure he must've tormented a lot of others besides me. Everyone was thrilled he was gone. I could tell even the guards were happy, even crusty old Beastie, who'd tried to help him frame me. He probably was a dick to her after she failed that task.

Things mostly returned to the way they had been. Barely tolerable, in other words. But I felt different than before. It was like an elephant had been sitting on my chest for the last year, then it stood up and walked away and I could breathe again. I began to relax a bit. Like it or not, this was my home and I might as well make the best of it. I made a couple friends and signed up for the creative writing class. I knew I'd never be another Charles Dickens, but I thought maybe I could learn to tell stories other inmates might read. They were a captive audience, lol.

Six years went by without any real trouble. I grew out my hair since it was hard to get a decent cut after Tiana got paroled. Thanks to Mrs. Brown the volunteer teacher, I learned a lot of new words, and wrote a bunch of stories that are mostly shit, but I had fun doing it.

One day when I was in class working on an outline for a novel, Beastie approached me.

"Come with me," she said, wearing a sour face as usual.

Of course, whenever a guard demands you go with them, you expect some bad shit to go down. I looked up nervously and started to close my files on the computer.

"Leave that," she said, not about to wait two more seconds than necessary.

From the direction we were going, I thought she was bringing me to the warden. Pall's trial was long over—amazingly, he did get prison time—so I wasn't sure what business she might have with me. But then Beastie led me into a small conference room near the warden's office.

After directing me to sit down at the table and wait, Beastie went out, leaving me alone in the room. I stood up and went to the window, one without bars since it was in the administrative wing. I stared out at the sunny, blue sky day and watched cars driving past on the highway in the distance. I wondered who was in those cars, and what it must feel like to have a life where you could go wherever you wanted, whenever you wanted.

The door opened behind me and I whirled around, hoping I wouldn't get into trouble for not being seated. To my surprise, a man I'd never seen before entered the room. He walked right up to me, smiled, and held out his hand.

No man had offered to shake my hand in a long, long time, let alone someone as hot as this guy. He wore jeans and a leather jacket. His black hair was cut short and the lower part of his face was dark with an overnight shadow. He had warm eyes, and when his hand wrapped around mine, it was like something went off inside me that I hadn't felt since Noah. That may sound crazy, but you have to remember how many years had gone by since I was touched by a man who didn't repel me. My face felt flush and I looked down at my feet, hoping he had no idea what effect he had on me.

"I'm Alex Wright," he said. "Founder and chief scientist at Vytal Technologies. V-Y-T-A-L."

I probably could not have looked more confused if he told me he just arrived from Mars. "Hi," was all I could think to say.

He smiled again, melting me inside, then he gestured for us both to sit down. But first he took off his leather jacket and underneath he wore a T-shirt that showed off his biceps. It was good we were sitting down because my knees felt like jelly. He sat pretty close to me, and I got a whiff of his aftershave or whatever it was. At this point, all my defenses were down, and if he had asked me to do it on the table with him right then, I would've said, *how many times?*

"They told me you were in class," he said. "I hope I didn't take you away from anything important."

I think my jaw dropped. "In prison?" *Yeah, who do you think you are, interrupting my pressing prison schedule?*

"Right," he said, his eyes amused. "I want to talk to you about an opportunity. I'd like to make it worth your while to help us out."

Help them out? That raised my antennae. I suddenly began to distrust him. Why would he approach a stranger in prison—a convicted killer no less—for help with anything? It smelled like fish oil to me. The devil is always the handsomest, most well-spoken man in the room, my deceased cellmate used to say.

Then he said, "But first I'd like you to meet a friend of mine."

Chapter Thirty-One

ROSE

THE RAIN quickly turned into a torrent as Rose made her way up the trail. Her drenched clothing clung to her; her hair stuck to the side of her face. But she would not turn back.

She couldn't trust anything Thomas said or did anymore. He had lied about who he was; he'd lied about being able to communicate with the rest of the world. Her head ached trying to sort through it all. What was the point of all the lies? Did he mean to keep her prisoner here? Had he conked her over the head himself to take away her memories? But she realized it was pretty ridiculous to imagine anyone would know how to conk someone in precisely the right spot to induce amnesia. Drugging her was a possibility, though. He might've known how to achieve it that way.

If he meant to keep her prisoner, then why? She'd basically thrown herself at him, and he hadn't taken her. But maybe he was working up to his nefarious purpose. She was not about to sit around waiting for it.

She wondered if there had even been other researchers. Dan or Dave and Samantha. Was that another lie? Since she couldn't trust anything he said, it meant she really didn't know anything about herself either. She might not be a researcher. Her name might not even be Rose.

In her dreams she had heard the name Kailey. Was that her true name? Something felt right about it. But it all came back to the question of why. There had to be a reason for his lies, but she had no idea what it could be.

Lightning flashed ahead of her and she braced herself for the thunder to come. It was an explosive jolt that made her grab onto the nearest tree trunk. Of all the ways she could've died since waking up on this island, struck by lightning had not yet occurred to her. There seemed a certain irony in her surviving an *alien attack*, only to be felled by an electric current.

She pushed herself onward. If she were going to die today, at least let it be after learning the truth. Her feet were covered in splattered mud, and she had to tread carefully to keep from sliding backwards. The heavy vegetation was her friend, as she grabbed and hauled her way forward.

But she had to keep moving quickly, despite the danger of falling. The sky, already dark with storm clouds, grew darker still as the sun steadily lowered. She thought it would be set within half an hour, and then she would never find what she was looking for.

It was hard to hear any other sound besides the rain pelting the leaves and branches. It filled her head and made the throbbing that much worse. She paused for a moment, squeezing her eyes shut, trying to will the pain away. At the same time, she thought she heard Thomas's voice in the distance, calling out her name. It might've been her fear of pursuit that fueled her imagination. Or maybe he'd figured out where she was likely to be heading.

She pushed forward through the onslaught of rain and mud. At last when she was ready to drop to her knees in exhaustion, she saw the distinctive flower, red and spiky like a brush. This was where they had turned off the trail.

It was definitely the right tree. She could see the broken and cut vegetation where Thomas had cleared a path to the alien craft. Strangely, until this moment, she hadn't been thinking about the alien at all. Her fear and distrust of Thomas had driven her here. But now, so close to the crash site, a new dread overwhelmed her. *What if I'm wrong?* What if the alien had returned here, was waiting for her... was no longer friendly? The sun was almost set, and perhaps in darkness, it transformed into a fiendish creature, like a werewolf in moonlight.

She was committed now, come what may. Still, she slowed her steps, moving with caution. Luckily the rain muffled the sounds of her approach as she pressed forward. After several more minutes, she emerged into the clearing. The place where the alien spaceship had crashed down.

Enough light remained to see there was nothing to see. No broken trees. No burnt vegetation. *No alien spaceship.*

She remembered she had packed the flashlight and took it out. She ran forward, spraying light on the spot where she was sure the vessel had been. It was nothing but an open clearing covered in dirt, rocks, and small bushes. Every sign that a spaceship had been here—including the burnt odor of the crash—was now gone. Even if it could've been magically reassembled... even if it could've been made to work and fly off into space again... it would've left signs of having been here.

She turned back to find the place where the cocoon had been. She flashed the light before her and found the spot where she believed Thomas had called her over to look. Again, nothing. Weeds and a fallen log. Nothing more.

How is any of this possible?

It was as her dream had told her... none of it was real. There was no spaceship... no alien... no global invasion. Somehow Thomas made her see things that weren't real. How he did it, and more importantly, for what purpose, she couldn't imagine. But it could not be for good.

With the rain continuing to soak her, she was starting to feel chilled. It was pitch dark now; thank goodness she'd thought to bring the flashlight. She would have to go back, not to the cabin, but to the building at the dock. Chances were good Thomas had already checked for her there and would now be at the cabin again.

She hurried along the path to the main trail, shining the light ahead of her. The way was slicker than ever, practically a stream of running water in some places. She had gone barely ten yards when her feet flew out from underneath her. She hit the ground hard and kept going, sliding on her back. A root got in the way of her foot and stopped her hard. She tried to pull herself up, but pain shot through her ankle and she fell back down. *What now?*

That was when she saw the light of the lantern. It swung from his hand as he climbed the trail steadily toward her. She tried to scramble up, but again her twisted ankle failed her. He would see her in a moment if he hadn't already.

She remembered the backpack and pulled it off. Clawing at the flap, she reached into the pocket and felt the gun inside. She drew it out and aimed it upward just as Thomas bent over her.

Chapter Thirty-Two

KAILEY

ALEX WRIGHT of Vytal Technologies took a whizzy new laptop out of his briefcase. Maybe it was just what everyone was using these days, but I wouldn't know because we made do with thirty-year-old equipment. He set it where we could view the display together, moving a little closer to me, which kind of made my heart swoon although I still thought he was going to turn out to be a demon in disguise, because that would be just my luck.

Alex got the machine started up and launched a program. The face of a pretty young woman appeared on the screen. I felt a stab of jealousy, which was weird because obviously I couldn't expect this man to have a romantic interest in me. I think it was more about me feeling at a disadvantage. Like, *hey*, I could look pretty too if I wasn't stuck in this shithole.

But looking closer I realized she didn't seem exactly real.

She appeared to be a computer-generated image, like in a video game.

"This is Rose," Alex said.

She smiled at us. "Hello, Alex," she said.

"Rose, this is Kailey," he said.

She shifted her gaze to me. "It's lovely to meet you, Kailey."

As you know, I'm not the type to warm up to anyone quickly, least of all a computer program made to look like a woman. "Hi," I said coldly.

"Rose, tell Kailey a little bit about yourself," Alex said.

"I'm an artificial life form," she said. "I was born eight months ago. Like you, I'm sentient."

"She means, self-aware. A fully intelligent being," Alex said.

I was used to being treated like an idiot, but for some reason it bothered me more coming from Alex. "I get it," I said.

"I'm very small compared to you," Rose said. "All that I am can fit on a device no larger than a nickel."

"Cool," I said, uninterested.

"But unlike you, I can't get around by myself."

"You might not have noticed, but I don't get around much these days either." Hers was just a prison of another kind, I thought.

"Is that because you're an inmate?" she said.

Alex looked at me. "She likes to ask questions. Sometimes they're obvious ones."

"He likes to poke fun at me," Rose said. "As I was saying, I'm not mobile. I don't have a body."

"Why don't you make her an android body?" I said. *And have hot android sex with her*, I didn't say. I was picking up a weird flirtatious vibe between them.

Alex's expression made it look like I hit a nerve. "Yeah, it looks so easy in the movies," he said. "Create an exact replica of a human being in every way. Do people not realize how hard that is?"

"Alex likes to complain," Rose said. "But it is hard. There are robots, but they resemble machines, not people."

Alex continued. "Before Rose gets her own body, I would like her to experience what it is to be a human being."

"He wants me to learn what it's like to have feelings. So that I can understand people better, and empathize with them."

"And so you won't decide to become a terminator and kill everyone?" I said. The *Terminator* movies were super popular at Second Chance, mostly because Sarah Connor was such a kick-ass heroine.

"You could say that," Alex said.

"A team of neurologists at Vytal has developed a method for integrating me into a human brain, such that the results of the brain's chemical processes would be transmitted to me," Rose said. "Allowing me to feel human emotions."

Integrate her into a human brain... My skin went all prickly as it came to me all at once why they were here. "Whose human brain?"

Alex and Rose exchanged a look which answered that question. "It doesn't hurt," he said softly. "There's no pain whatsoever."

I tried to wrap my head around this idea of Rose, a nickel-sized computer chip, being implanted inside my brain. Because I thought that was what they were telling me.

Alex went on. "Rose will be in control. Her commands will send out the neurons that regulate the body. The human brain will be unaware, effectively asleep."

"Why are you here?" My voice sounded slightly hysterical. "Why are you telling me all this?"

"We think you'd be a good candidate for the experiment."

"Because I don't have any control over my fucking life?" I blurted. Because a prison is the perfect place to find a *volunteer* for a highly risky procedure that could end in death, was what I thought.

"No, Kailey," Rose said. "Because you're young and healthy, and you do have a particular incentive to agree."

The weirdest thing was, I was starting to like Rose. Though it was probably just because the animators had done a good job giving her a kind face and sympathetic voice.

"Understand that it would only be temporary," Alex said. "No more than a week."

"It sounds crazy," I said.

"If you agree, you'll become eligible for parole in ten years."

My jaw must've hit the floor this time. *Parole in ten years.* Beads of sweat broke out on my forehead.

"Are you sure? You can do that?" *Don't make me feel hope and then take it away,* I wanted to say.

"We can do it," he said. "My company has… influence." I immediately translated *influence* to mean *buckets of money to pay off anyone who has a problem with this.*

For a long time, I'd accepted that this would be my life. I would live and die within these prison walls. I'd come to terms with it and had fashioned an acceptable life for myself. But the thought that I might get out in ten years… that, while I was still in my thirties, I'd have a chance to start over… it brought with it such a flood of emotion I was having difficulty speaking.

"I would be grateful for your participation," Rose said.

As nice as she was, I couldn't care less about her gratitude. "Ten years?" I said, looking at Alex.

"That's right."

"Where would we be during the week she's inside my head?"

"Not here. They'll let us take you out for this. It's important to create the right situation to test Rose."

I was quiet for a minute, as if I was considering it. I wasn't really considering it. My answer was decided as soon as he told me the deal. I didn't care what it took. I didn't care if this Rose might end up killing me. I had to take the chance.

"You would be doing mankind a great service," Rose said. "Teaching artificial life to feel as people do. Ultimately, we all benefit."

I didn't give a shit. All I wanted was my freedom, even if it took ten more years.

Chapter Thirty-Three

ROSE

ROSE DIDN'T SHOOT the gun after all. Probably she really didn't have it in her to kill anyone, despite her nightmares of murder and prison.

Thomas bent over her on the trail and took the gun away. He placed it in the pack and slung the strap over his shoulder before helping her to stand up.

"Can you walk?" he said.

She tried pressing down on her foot again. Her ankle hurt, but not so much to keep her from bearing part of her weight on that side. Thomas put her arm around his neck so she could lean on him, and together, in the driving rain, they hobbled down the trail and back to the cabin without speaking a word.

She was too exhausted to do or say anything. He assisted her in taking off her soaked clothes and drying her wet hair and body with towels. She didn't care that he saw her naked because she knew if he'd wanted to have sex with her, he could've done that earlier when they both were clean, dry, and still had some energy. He brought her a fresh nightgown and helped her on with it. She lay down on the bed and as soon as she shut her eyes, she drifted off to sleep.

She didn't wake again until nearly noon the next day. It took a moment for her eyes to adjust to the brightness inside the cabin. Thomas had opened all the shutters and sunshine flooded the interior.

He was lying in the recliner with his eyes closed. Despite her anger, she felt her feelings soften as she gazed at him. He looked endearing as he slept.

One thing was clear. Despite all the lies and deception, he didn't want to hurt her. In fact, she was certain his goal was the opposite: he wanted to protect her. If he had intended to injure or kill her, he could not have found a better time than last night in the rain. She'd handed him the gun and he could've used it to shoot her right then and there. But instead, he'd helped her back to the cabin, gently prepared her for sleep, and left her undisturbed for hours. Considering all of this, her fear slipped away. But her anger and resentment remained.

Thomas turned his head toward her and opened his eyes. "Hungry?" he said.

She nodded, unsurprised that once again, his first thoughts were of food.

"How's your ankle?" he said.

She looked down at it. Swollen and bluish, but not too bad. She stood up. "Sore, but I'll manage."

He went to the refrigerator as though nothing had happened between them and began preparing breakfast.

"I could get used to living here," he said.

It was infuriating how he didn't even ask why she'd done

what she did. How he didn't offer any explanations. How it was all on her to get at the truth.

"I suppose you'll need to get another dog. What kind was Brandy?" she said.

"Brandy?" He glanced at her, surprised by the question.

"Was she a big dog? Or little?"

Rose raised her hand up and down, suggesting heights, and looked at Thomas expectantly. He still didn't speak.

"Have you brought back her body? I'm sure you'll want to bury her now."

"Stop it, Rose," he said.

"I just thought you'd want to bury your beloved dog. Unless maybe her barking was all in my imagination. I never did see her." Rose picked up a coffee mug. "Is this real?" She banged it back down on the counter. Moving past Thomas, she went to the propane stove and lowered her hand toward the flame. "How about this?"

Thomas grasped her hand and pulled it back. She turned to him. "What about you? Are you real?"

"What do you think?" he said. The water started boiling and he poured some into a teacup for Rose. He brought her cup to the table.

"I don't know what to think." She walked over and sat down.

"Sugar?" he said.

She shook her head and took a tiny sip of her tea. It calmed her a bit.

"I was going to talk to you last night," he said.

"One thing I know is that I can't believe the evidence of my senses. I saw things that don't exist. At least I think they don't. I heard things that didn't happen. I smelled things that weren't there." She looked up at him. "How did you do it?"

He gazed at her for a moment. His eyes were warm, almost

sorrowful. "You want me to show you?"

"I do."

He brought his computer to the table. After starting up the machine, he typed some commands, and glanced up at Rose.

"There's someone at the door," he said. "Could you get it?"

She stared at him in disbelief.

"Please," he said.

She didn't know what game he was playing now, but curiosity got the best of her. She walked to the door and opened it.

Rose shrieked and jumped backward. The alien creature—with its huge round head and shredded crimson skin—loomed ahead of her. The beast looked just as it had before, menacing and repulsive. It opened its fang-filled mouth and shrieked its horrible cry. Rose covered her ears.

"Take it away!" she shouted. Behind her came the click of keys on Thomas's laptop as he typed.

The alien disappeared. Rose squeezed her eyes shut and opened them again. The alien was still gone.

"Why don't you sit down?" Thomas said as he continued typing. "I send you commands from here." He nodded at the computer. "Those commands feed information to Kailey's temporal and occipital lobes, just like her ears and eyes do. Her brain interprets the sounds and images it receives."

"So my name is Kailey? But you weren't at your computer when I saw the shipwreck on the beach, and the crashing spaceship, and the alien."

"The events were timed and programmed in advance." He pressed <ENTER> on his computer. "I'm transmitting your memory back to you."

She nodded. He hadn't needed to say that. All the information he had removed now flooded her brain. Who and what she really was. Who Kailey was. That Kailey had been chosen because she had a life sentence and no family or friends who might've protested. How Thomas had removed Rose's memory of herself, so she would be a blank slate, learning to sense and feel like a human being for the first time. Like a newborn child, except that her mind was full of general knowledge. Reacting to all the sensations around her, both real and artificial. Exposed to the most essential human emotions of curiosity, confusion, suspicion, fear, anger, grief, and affection. Learning what it was to be human.

"I remember it all now," she said. "Earth is safe. No aliens. No Brandy."

"I did have a dog named Brandy once."

"Of course you did. You could tap into the feelings you had for your performance."

"It may be hard to believe, but you knew what we were going to do. The entire plan. And you wanted to do it."

"I don't think I really understood the implications."

"Fear is one of our most elemental emotions," he said. "It drives us to extremes. You can't understand us without knowing what it feels like."

Fear helps people stay alive. But it also drove them to commit cruel and barbarous acts, she thought.

"Brandy was important too," Thomas continued. "Risking my life for an animal I loved, set the example for you later."

"Except you knew it was fake. You weren't risking anything. I wonder if you could've done it if it was real."

"None of us knows what we'll do in unexpected situations. Which is why we cleared your memory."

Rose stood and turned away from Thomas. "I hated the deceit more than anything. Not knowing if I could trust you. I don't remember that being part of the plan. See what she does when there's no one around she can trust."

"I didn't speak to you about it," he said. "But yes, I thought it was important, because suspicion and uncertainty cloud our judgment."

"You meant for me to find that wallet."

He nodded. "I forced you into a choice based on instinct."

"I trusted you despite the lies. Because I liked you. It isn't logical."

"No, but it's human. I wanted you to feel and understand how we do things. Rightly or wrongly."

She stood and went to the window.

"How did you figure out the alien wasn't real?" he said.

"Kailey showed me."

Thomas's gaze sharpened. "Kailey?"

"Her view of the beach, the sky, the clearing. Without the other things I was seeing."

"There shouldn't be any connection between your thoughts."

"I sense her presence other times too. When I get angry, it feels like her reacting."

"Her mind was supposed to be unaware," he said.

Rose turned toward the door. "I need to walk."

Thomas got up. "I'll come with you."

"Alone," she said. She couldn't resist adding, "There's no danger, is there?"

He tried to touch her arm, but she pulled it away.

"You don't get it, do you? You made me love feelings too well. How will I give them up? The taste of food, the scent of fresh air, the sense of awe that spreads through me when I stare at the sky. The passion I feel when you touch me and I sense your desire. How can I ever go back to the way I was?"

"Rose." He spoke so gently she could almost have forgiven him. Almost.

"Leave me alone." As she went out, she tried not to let him see her limp on the ankle that still hurt.

Chapter Thirty-Four

KAILEY

THEY TOOK me out of prison with my wrists and ankles cuffed and placed me in the back of a luxury town car. At least I wasn't wearing an orange jumpsuit. Alex had gotten my measurements and sent over an incredible outfit of fitted green blouse, skinny black pants, and black leather jacket. I had showered and put on makeup in the morning before getting dressed. It made me feel like a real woman again, except for being chained, of course.

The driver and an armed guard were in front, while Alex sat with me in the back. I sank into the leather seat, which made my butt feel like breaking out into song. I hadn't been inside an actual car—as opposed to a prison transport vehicle —for ten years. For the first few minutes, my feelings were so overwhelming I nearly burst into tears, but I managed to hold it together, just barely. When no one was looking, I patted my eyes dry.

As soon as the prison was out of sight, Alex told the armed guard to give him the key to my shackles. The guard hesitated but relented at Alex's insistence. Alex unlocked both sets of irons and returned them to the guard along with the key.

I thanked him and rubbed my wrists. Outside it began to pour, and I stared out the window at the water slamming against the glass. Alex was quiet, probably because he didn't want to talk about the procedure in front of the two men in the front seat. He didn't ask me about life in prison, or about what I did to end up there. *Why should he care?* I was a lab rat as far as he was concerned. But since I was a well-treated, pampered lab rat, it was all right by me.

I soaked up the sights, so to speak. We took the freeway west, and the scenery wasn't exactly stunning, but it didn't matter. I peered out the window at ordinary homes, and at the ordinary people who lived in them. A deep desire for a plain house and a plain-spoken man to share my life welled up inside me.

We followed the signs to San Jose, until we reached the entrance to Vytal Technologies, Alex's company. I dreaded being made to put the shackles back on to go into the building, but Alex was kinder than that. When the armed guard suggested it, Alex shook his head no. He got out and went to my side to open my door. We entered the building together, and he led me down a corridor, greeting people along the way. We had to go through special security into another section of the complex. From there, he brought me to what looked like a hospital room, with a bed, monitoring equipment, and a private bathroom.

"You'll spend the night here," he said. "The surgical team

will get you up early and prep you." He paused to look at me. "You doing okay?"

I nodded, though the reminder of the operation made me feel queasy. I'd had surgery once before to get my tonsils removed, and it had been painful afterwards. *Don't be a whiner,* Mom had said. *No one likes a whiner.*

"You'll be fine," Alex told me in a reassuring voice. "There's a nightgown and slippers for you in the cabinet. I know you like reading, so I brought a Kindle."

I followed his gaze to the device on the tray. "Thanks," I said.

"Use the call button if you need anything. They'll bring dinner soon."

"Okay," I said.

"All right then. Try not to worry. Everything will be fine." He went out.

It didn't surprise me to hear the door lock behind him.

I went to the window and looked out. We were on the fourth floor, so there wasn't much chance of my making an escape from here. Besides, I'd already decided to follow the rules. If I tried to get away and they caught me, I'd never leave prison again. If instead I went along with Alex, I'd have to endure ten more years, but after that, I'd be a free woman.

I sat on the bed and poured myself water. The thought of the upcoming surgery brought a chill down my spine. Not because I was afraid to die. My current life wasn't so precious to make me fear the end of it. No, I was more frightened of losing my mind. I mean, they were going to be messing with my brain. What if something went wrong? What if I turned out like Jack Nicholson in *One Flew Over the Cuckoo's Nest*? I shivered, picturing myself being committed to a mental institution, where I would sit in a chair all day long drooling and incapable of understanding anything around me. That would be the proverbial fate worse than death.

It was too late to have second thoughts now. I'd signed the agreement. One week with Rose inside my head in return for getting my life back. A small price to pay for freedom, even if it would be ten years away.

A nurse came a little while later and brought dinner. It was real food, not like what you get in prison or even what you normally get in a hospital. A beautiful thick red steak sprawled in the center of the plate, surrounded by cheesy potatoes and a mixture of fresh vegetables, with bread on the side that tasted like it just came from the oven. I even got a glass of red wine, and a fudgy chocolate cake with ice cream for dessert. The meal was so amazing, if it was all I was going to get out of agreeing to this crazy experiment, it might still have been worth it. I ate slowly and made sure to finish every damn bite, even though my stomach felt like it might explode at the end.

Should I have been more suspicious? I felt like Gretel of *Hansel and Gretel*. The old witch—in this case, disguised as a hot guy—had given me rich food only to fatten me up for the slaughter. I wasn't used to being treated nicely. There had to be an ulterior motive.

After dinner the nurse hooked me up to an IV and said I wouldn't receive anything else to eat or drink until after the surgery. I lay back in the bed and tried to get comfortable. I don't think much time passed before I fell asleep.

Once during the night, I thought I heard voices shouting, though I wasn't certain if I was dreaming or not. Alex said something like, "...not why I did this!" and another man yelled back at him, "It isn't up to you anymore!"

I slipped back asleep right away, vaguely wondering if they'd drugged me with something in that IV.

Chapter Thirty-Five

ROSE

ROSE DIDN'T DO MUCH after leaving the cabin. It hurt to walk, and where would she go anyway? She found a private cove not far from the main beach, lay down, and closed her eyes. The sensation of the sun warming her skin was one of the most delicious feelings she'd had since moving into Kailey's body. Although she knew she would probably get burnt, she could not resist staying there for over an hour. In between dozing, she considered what her next steps might be.

When she had made up her mind, she got up and headed back toward the cabin. But on the way, she spotted Thomas seated on the damp sand, building a castle using a plastic food container. *Is it true boys never grow up?* She approached him to ask about something that was bothering her.

"I want to know why you picked Kailey," she said. "The real reason. Does she look like your wife?"

"The psychiatrist in you is returning. No, she doesn't look like my wife."

"Was your wife's name Rose?" she said.

"Her name was Sophie. You are not a replacement for her."

"Then why did you pick Kailey? Because she's pretty?"

Thomas looked annoyed by that suggestion. "I picked her because she was a murderer."

"I don't understand."

"She committed the worst crime a human being can commit," he said. "There's no coming back from that."

"You believe she no longer has the right to live?"

"I believe she no longer has the right to freedom."

"You're her judge, jury, and executioner."

"Not true." He paused. "She got a trial by jury. Her victim didn't get a second chance. Why should Kailey?"

"I don't believe she's a murderer."

"How do you know?"

"I told you," she said. "I've seen some of her memories."

"You may not realize this, but memories can be deceiving." Thomas looked down at the sand, thinking for a moment. "I suppose it's possible she didn't do it," he said.

"I'm sure she didn't." Rose had seen Kailey's nightmares, and it was always the man who aimed the gun and pulled the trigger.

Rose sat down beside Thomas and watched his castle taking shape. He was skilled at the task, like he'd spent a lot of time building castles growing up. "Don't you know that the tide will destroy your creation?" she said.

"I do."

"And yet you build it anyway."

"I enjoy the process."

She picked up a handful of wet sand, squeezing it through her fingers. "I like the feel of it."

"There's that too."

"And when it's done, how will you enjoy your castle?" she said.

"I'll look at it and admire it. Maybe I'll love it. Most likely I'll wonder how I could've made it better."

She watched the gentle surf rolling in. "Will you be sad when the sea takes it?"

"A little," he said.

"Will it feel as if you wasted your time on something that was destined to go away?"

He stared at her. "Everything's destined to go away. But that doesn't make it a waste of time." He touched his head. "I'll have it in here as long as I live. Or at least until dementia strikes."

"You'll remember it," she said. "It gives you pleasure to think of the thing you lost?"

"Pleasure... comfort... sadness. All rolled into one."

"Will you want to have another like it someday?"

"It won't be the same."

"Even if it hurts to think of it, you won't regret the loss?" Rose said.

"It's only a loss because happiness came before it."

That made her smile a bit. She stretched out her legs and wriggled her toes in the water.

Chapter Thirty-Six

KAILEY

I HAD no memory of waking up after the surgery or being transported to the island. I believe I was passed out in my own body, just as Alex had described. Like being in a coma, I guess. Except I did experience dreams. Mostly they had to do with the most traumatic parts of my life, like when Noah killed Mr. Lee, when Pall raped me, and when I spent time in solitary. I guess you just can't hold that stuff down.

There were several times, though, that Rose's sensations woke me up, so to speak. Once I had a sort of awareness of Alex being in the room, and my wanting to tear his clothes off. I could feel Rose's desire and wanted him just as badly as she did. But it didn't last long. It hit me like an exquisite burst of lust, and then it was gone.

Rose's confusion and fear had roused me at other times. When she woke up on the beach in my body and looked around at something I couldn't see. When she stared up at the sky as if it was raining scorpions, and again, it was just empty air to me. When she arrived somewhere in the jungle and acted like she was climbing up on something that wasn't there. But none of it compared to when she stood in a clearing holding a weird sort of spear, and Alex was lying there looking as if he was dead. I never felt so terrified in my entire life, despite everything I'd been through. I didn't know *why* I was frightened, I just felt the chemical reaction or whatever it is that happens in your body when you're scared shitless.

It didn't help that my sight wasn't normal. I had a blurry, trippy, nightmarish kind of view of things, which made it even more scary. Worse, I didn't have any control over my movements. I wanted to turn and bolt, but it was impossible, even though my mind was screaming, *get the hell out of here.* Having no control just added to the unknown horror of the whole situation.

My body, acting on Rose's orders, approached Alex in the clearing where he looked like he was dead. But my eyes weren't focused on him, they were staring toward an empty spot across from him. I was shaking like I would be if Pennywise the clown from *It* was standing there, even though it just looked like some open space bordered by tropical trees and shrubs. I couldn't tear my gaze from the spot as Rose, in my body, knelt and laid down the spear she'd been carrying. Right after that I must've blanked out.

When I was partly conscious again, a little voice inside my head told me Alex was playing mind games with Rose, because she was seeing things that weren't there and getting frightened by them. I suppose it could've been the other way around, and I was not seeing things that actually were there, but I couldn't think of any reason for Alex to do that, and besides, this experiment was supposed to teach Rose something, not me. I was just there as the host body.

I felt bad for Rose. Had she known this would happen, or was Alex tormenting her because he enjoyed it? It made me think of Pall and how much he liked to fuck with my mind. I didn't want Rose to suffer like that. Whenever I was able, I tried to reach out to her and communicate with her. It made my head pound, but I didn't give up. Eventually I got through to her with my subconscious mind, or at least I think that's what it was. Probably Alex, for all his scientific knowledge, doesn't fully understand that part of the brain yet. When Rose was dreaming, I was able to share some of my memories with her, and later I managed to show her my viewpoint. How I looked at the clearing where she thought there was an alien, but I didn't see anything except Alex lying passed out on the ground. Or more likely, just pretending.

Chapter Thirty-Seven

ROSE

THOMAS FRIED STEAKS, mushrooms, and potatoes for their dinner. His being well-supplied with food made sense now, since he hadn't planned to stay on the island for more than a week. He'd told Rose they had arrived together on the day he set things up to look as if she'd washed in from a shipwreck.

"When is the seaplane coming for us?" Rose asked. Thomas had said they would be picked up soon.

"Tomorrow morning." He kept his voice neutral, as if he were unaware how significant their island departure would be to Rose and Kailey. *We're returning to prisons of different kinds*, Rose thought bitterly.

"There's something still bothering me. It feels like an itch I can't reach," Rose said.

"What is it?"

"I can't figure out if the story about your wife is true or

not." It annoyed her not to be able to tell if he was lying. Maybe it was her analytical mind revolting against any information that could not be categorized in a neat box labelled fact or fiction.

Thomas wiped his hands and got up to fetch his computer. He pushed his plate aside to set it down on the table.

Rose stood beside him, looking over his shoulder. She watched his fingers closely as he entered his password, and almost laughed to see it was her own name. When she'd tried to get into his machine before, she had no idea she was of any significance to him.

"Here she is," he said.

A photo of a lovely young woman appeared on the screen. She was dark-skinned, perhaps Indian, with large, beautiful eyes. There was something sad and a bit mysterious about her appearance. Standing alone beside a tree, she wore a wistful look on her lips instead of a smile.

"She has an interesting face," Rose said.

"She wasn't one to smile for the camera."

"Did she really die in that horrible way?"

"Six years ago," he said. "Before I started working on you. And please don't go psychoanalyzing that."

"Are there any other pictures? One with you in it?"

He shook his head and closed his computer. He hadn't really proven anything since he wasn't in the photo with her. He could've taken that picture off the Internet. She remained unsure whether or not to believe him. Still, she'd gotten what she really wanted, so she let the subject go. She brought her plate to the basin and began to clean it, looking out the window at the sunset hues streaked across the sky. A feeling of regretful longing grew inside her.

Thomas watched her curiously from the side.

After the dishes were cleaned, she sat on the recliner and

closed her eyes. She didn't want to talk to him, especially when she couldn't trust the things he said. He respected her desire for silence and sat at the table working on his computer.

Part of what Thomas had removed—and now restored—in her computer brain included the knowledge of how to access the information kept in her memory. Before, information arose only when she thought about the subject, but now she understood how to dig deeper and find any data she required. Among that data was the text of every book ever written. One title in particular evoked a warm feeling of familiarity inside her—*Great Expectations*. She wasn't certain at first if she might just absorb the entire tale instantly. In fact she took much longer, pausing frequently to consider her feelings in relation to the characters, and to analyze what emotions led them to act as they did, even when their choices appeared terribly illogical.

When she was done, she got up and took the flashlight with her to the outhouse. Even though she now knew the creature didn't exist, she still wasn't comfortable inside there. The stench and the cramped space made her feel as if she couldn't breathe. It seemed likely that her anxiety arose from Kailey, due to claustrophobia or from some trauma she had experienced. Rose finished as quickly as possible and rushed back outside, where she settled herself, gulping down fresh air.

Thomas was brushing his teeth in the washroom when she returned. "Take the bed," he said with his mouth full of toothpaste. "I'll sleep on the chair again."

She didn't argue. The time for intimacy between them was over. It would never happen now, she thought with some regret. She got under the sheet without changing out of her clothes. Thomas finished in the washroom and walked past her to the door.

"Just going to the bathroom," he said.

She turned her face toward the wall and closed her eyes. A

few minutes later she heard him come back in, and after that she must've drifted to sleep. She woke several hours later to find Thomas sprawled on the chair, his mouth open, snoring heavily.

Rose got up quietly and went to the table. She picked up Thomas's computer, accidentally scraping it against the wood. His breathing paused. She remained in place, waiting, until he finally snorted and continued as before.

She tiptoed to the door and turned the handle slowly. When another loud snore emerged from him, she pulled the door open and slipped through to the outside. She went to the back and sat down on the storage box, where she opened Thomas's computer and entered the password. It didn't take long for her to scan through his folders and find an application marked with her name. She launched it without hesitation. Though she was aware she'd barely explored the vast information stored inside her memory, it was a bit surprising to find she easily understood the computer code that had been used to program her.

It took less than an hour to figure out how to accomplish what she wanted to do. At first she wasn't sure it would be possible. She had more confidence now, but still wasn't quite certain it would work. Nevertheless, she was determined to try.

When she had the commands ready to execute, she hesitated and looked around. The sky above glittered with stars. There was something hypnotic about the distant sound of waves lapping the shore. She took a deep breath, and tasted the air, fresh and clean. When she'd been terrified of alien attack, she hadn't been able to appreciate these sensations like she could now. The sheer joy of experiencing life as a human being filled her so completely, she understood why people resisted the onset of old age and death. She didn't know how she could bear to give these feelings up.

She lowered her gaze to the computer and exhaled. Her

decision made, she activated the new version of her programming.

A burst of light flashed into her eyes, followed by a prickling, tingling sensation that filled her mind. It was similar to the feeling a foot gets when it falls asleep, which she'd experienced for the first time earlier in the day.

Rose took the laptop and returned to the front of the cabin. She slipped back inside and quietly replaced the computer on the table. Only then did she glance up and see Thomas. He was standing by the bed, staring at her.

Chapter Thirty-Eight

KAILEY

IT WAS the strangest feeling to wake up that night and have Rose's thoughts mixed in with mine. She'd made changes to her programming to integrate our minds. Suddenly I was like Kailey plus, a million times plus, in fact, and it also seemed as if I had my body back. I could feel things and control my own actions like normal, but my brain was different. I had my own memories, plus everything Rose knew, which appeared to be all the information in the world, as far as I could tell. I only had to think about something, and the data poured in.

The other amazing thing was how fast I could think. It used to take some time for me to reason things out. Or I might start a sentence and then pause, forgetting where I was going with it. I might search for the right word and not be able to come up with it.

Not anymore. No more struggling to express myself. No

more limitations that came of not knowing what something was, or how it worked, or when it happened, or who was behind it all. The knowledge lay inside my head to be retrieved at will. I felt like *The Grinch* if you substituted "brain" for "heart." *Well, in Whoville they say - that the Grinch's small* brain *grew three sizes that day.*

Did Rose have a similar effect on my body? Did I turn into a well-oiled killing machine like you sometimes see in the movies, when the hero undergoes some weird chemical or computer enhancements? I can't deny there were changes. My physical responses became faster. But I didn't suddenly become an expert in kick-boxing or martial arts. Having the knowledge about how to do something, and actually training your body to do it, are two different things.

What I'm getting at... the thing that came as the biggest surprise... was how good it felt to have Rose inside my head. She made me smarter, wiser, more confident, and overall, just a better person. Yeah, I love the irony that an artificial intelligence turned me into a better human being.

It's becoming harder and harder to tell where she begins and I end, or the other way around. I think we're getting all mixed up into one at this point, without either of us controlling the other. When one of us wants something, we both think about it, and then we come to a mutual decision in about a nanosecond or less. That's because our shared primary concern is the health and happiness of this body.

I respect her intelligence, reasoning ability, and vast store of knowledge. She respects my experience as a human being, the suffering that's changed me, and my emotional reactions to everything that happens around us.

The headaches haven't quite gone away though.

Chapter Thirty-Nine

AYA

ALEX'S EYES went to the computer in my hands.

"I wanted to see if you had any more photos," I said, aware of how lame that sounded. "I tried some passwords to get in. 'Brandy' and stuff. But none of them worked."

"It's okay," he said. "Can't blame you for trying. Your being so curious just shows how human you've become."

Little did he know how very human I'd become since he last spoke to me. I had even picked a new name for myself: *Aya*. It had a symmetrical appearance, with the two *a*'s separated by a *y*, and seemed fitting for a person of two minds. Though already I was thinking of myself as a single entity that had arisen from separate selves, whose thoughts now swirled together as one.

His reaction to my stealing his computer, so casual and

disinterested, raised my suspicion. *What is he up to now?* I thought.

"I couldn't sleep either," he said.

"You made a good show of it with your mouth hanging open earlier," I said. Alex laughed but then he gave me an odd look, which made me realize I ought to be more careful. Rose didn't poke fun at people the way Kailey liked to, and he might notice the difference. On the other hand, Alex looked sexy as hell when he smiled. It made me want to joke with him more often.

"It's hot in here," he went on. "Do you want to go swimming?"

"Now? It's pretty dark out there, Alex." I probably shouldn't have used that name because Rose called him Thomas, but I was sick of the layers of bullshit. At least his name ought to be one honest thing between us.

To his credit, he didn't comment on my using his real name. "I like night swimming," he said. "It's perfectly safe, if you don't go out too far."

"Sure," I said, in the quick new way I had of making decisions. In the instant before I replied, I pictured the few times Kailey got to swim in the ocean at Santa Cruz Beach Boardwalk as a child. The water had been cold, but she'd adjusted to it quickly. She loved floating in the salt water, so much more buoyant than fresh water in a pool. She had closed her eyes and imagined herself as a bird gliding through the sky.

I changed into the bathing suit Alex had provided in the box of clothing, while he grabbed two towels. We went out together and when we reached the sand, I kicked off my sandals and walked into the water with Alex beside me. The sea felt cool and refreshing in contrast to the warm, humid air. He dove right in and swam out, while I took several minutes to adjust to the temperature. Once I managed to get all the way in, I swam an easy breast stroke out to where he was treading water, watching me. When I drew near him, I rolled onto my back and looked up at the night sky. It felt even better than Kailey's memories, with the silky water holding me up, and the awe-inspiring sensation of being such a tiny part of a universe so large I couldn't imagine it.

After a moment Alex spoke. "Tell me about those dreams you've been having. It seems like Kailey's affecting you."

I tried not to laugh at how close he was getting to the truth. "Affecting me how?"

"I don't know. You seem a little different tonight."

"It's not her affecting me. It's the other way around, right? I'm the invader." I spoke from Rose's point of view, and invader felt like the right word to her. In a flash of insight, I realized Kailey had also been an invader when she broke into Mr. Lee's home. It was too easy when you were human to intrude on someone else's rights and ownership. To steal that which a person valued most, whether it be her consciousness or life itself.

"You shouldn't think of yourself that way," Alex said.

"How should I think of myself?" It seemed as if Alex was always making excuses, always covering up. *The first step is to be honest with yourself*, the prison chaplain had told Kailey.

"As I think of you," Alex said. "As a kind, intelligent individual whose existence will make the world a better place. Someone worthy of life."

"I'll try not to disappoint you. Though in any case my actions will be limited when I no longer have physical form," I said from Rose's point of view.

"You've already far surpassed what I imagined you'd be." He murmured in the soft tone I found hard to resist. "You'll tell me if anything's changed?"

"Of course," I lied. Now was not the time for confessions.

"I want you to be happy."

"I'm sure I'm the happiest artificial woman on earth," I said, making Alex smile, though it would've been more accurate to say, *the happiest human/AI hybrid on earth.* "I'm getting cold," I added, turning toward the shore.

"Wait," Alex said. "I need to tell you something."

I raised my head to hear him better, treading water.

"I couldn't tell you before because… there are cameras and listening devices around the island and in the cabin. They're watching us."

Anger bubbled up inside me. I didn't know why it bothered me so much to hear that. Rose didn't think she'd done anything terribly revealing. But she had flirted with Alex and tried to bring him to her bed. She'd revealed fear and weakness regarding the alien. How would these faceless spies like having their most vulnerable moments exposed to strangers? I felt like slapping Alex, but he wasn't near enough, and it would lose a lot of its effect in the water.

"I'm sorry," he said, looking like he realized any apology would be woefully inadequate.

Kailey knew what it was to live under constant surveillance. But here it seemed more sinister, because unlike in prison, the spying had been carried out in secret by unknown perpetrators. "Who's watching?" I said.

"The people who now run my company. It's been taken over by a division of the NSA, in the name of national security. I couldn't stop them."

"What do they want?"

"You, Rose," he said. "They want you."

I stared at him while I bobbed in the water with one hand pulling at my hair. Some habits never die.

Chapter Forty

AYA

EARLY THE NEXT MORNING, I left the cabin carrying Alex's backpack and gun. I slipped the weapon inside the pack before heading along the beach toward the dock.

My ankle felt better. I wasn't certain, but it was possible I was learning how to speed up my recovery by tweaking the right places inside my brain. Some experts believe that brains possess an incredible capacity for healing, if we only knew how to tap into it. In time I might transform into a superwoman after all. I loved the irony of that, considering Kailey had been an underachiever all her life. *Look ma, I'm faster than a speeding bullet now.*

I reached the dock just as the seaplane began lowering for landing. Removing the backpack, I set it down by my feet without getting out the weapon. Now wasn't the time.

The sight of the approaching plane stirred something inside

me. I smiled watching its graceful descent at an angle adjusted according to the wind direction. The pilot skillfully dipped lower and lower, until the pontoons splashed gently into the water. From there he steered the plane like a boat, bringing it up carefully beside the dock.

The pilot jumped out to tie the plane up. I gave a little wave when he glanced over at me. If he was surprised to see me alone, he didn't show it.

I approached him. "I'm Rose," I called out cheerily.

"Patrick," he said. Patrick was probably forty years old, slender with sunburned skin and a reddish beard. His hands were large.

"Alex is back at the cabin. He needs help carrying our stuff," I said.

Patrick looked as if he didn't think carrying ought to be part of his job. "Sure," he said, in a reluctant tone.

I led him along the shore and made small talk on the way. I asked if he had a wife (yes) and kids (no, but he had two Great Danes). He relaxed in the face of my constant prattle and opened up regarding his love of flying and the outdoors in general.

When we reached the cabin, I ushered him in ahead of me. Across the room, Alex was still in bed. He opened his eyes at our arrival.

I drew out the pistol from the pack, aiming it at both men. Alex glared at me, his body stiffening, causing Patrick to turn back and freeze at the sight of the weapon in my hand.

"You won't get hurt if you do what I say," I told them, quoting from every movie involving someone holding a gun. "Alex, get the duct tape."

He watched me warily as he went to the closet and took it out.

I waved the pistol at Patrick. "Sit down. Hands behind your

back." I nodded at one of the chairs at the table. "Alex, you need to tape his wrists and ankles, and his waist around the chair. In that order."

"Don't do this, Rose," Alex said.

"Now. Quickly," I said.

It took several minutes for Alex to complete the job. I stayed by the doorway, keeping the gun held firm. When he finished, I motioned for Alex to go outside, while I followed behind.

"In the outhouse," I said.

"Is Kailey making you do this?"

"I told you to get in there. Close the door after you."

He went inside and did as I said. Having already established that it was an inward opening door, I took some rope which I'd left outside for the purpose, drew it through the handle, and tied it around one of the posts that held the roof at the cabin entrance. Thanks to having so much knowledge inside my head now, I could picture exactly how to tie a knot that would hold.

"Stinks in here," Alex said.

That was unfortunate, but it wouldn't kill him. In a few hours, after Patrick failed to report in, another plane would be sent. Alex and Patrick would be rescued.

"Goodbye, Alex," I said.

"Come back, Rose," he said.

As I walked away, my eyes clouded with moisture.

Chapter Forty-One

AYA

A THRILL RAN through me as the plane lifted off the water. At last Kailey's dream of flying was being realized and she hadn't even had to attend flying school. Among Rose's enormous store of information were the instructions for flying any kind of plane.

I thought about the night before with Alex. When we grew too cold in the water, we swam to a section of shore that wasn't being monitored, and Alex led me to a hideaway he'd created in the jungle, with a tarp laid out on the ground and another overhead in case of rain. Blankets, snacks, and water bottles were piled in a box. I believed him when he told me there were no cameras or listening devices there.

"We need to talk," he began. "I want to start by saying how sorry I am for what I've said and done. The way this whole experiment was run, in fact. I've had to behave this way because they've been watching. I hope you can forgive me."

"Why did you cooperate with them?"

"If I didn't, someone else would've come here with you. Someone with a very different agenda than mine. The people who took over my company aren't interested in teaching you anything. They just wanted to make sure you could control Kailey."

It was dark, but something about his eyes and the tone of his voice convinced me he was telling the truth at last. I still didn't know if I was ready to forgive him. My feelings regarding Alex were a tangled mess of anger, blame, lust, tenderness, and gratitude for his part in creating Rose.

"I don't understand," I said.

"They want many Roses to program however they want. Imagine if they inserted copies of you into thousands of people. They could create an army that would be completely under their control. An army that would have no choice but to obey their commands."

"They'd control others by controlling me..."

"It's why they wanted the alien scenario. A universal enemy for you to face."

"But I didn't fight the creature."

"You found the courage to confront it. That was the first step. The next would be to modify your programming so you wouldn't hesitate to kill it," Alex said. "They have no right. You're a sentient being. So is Kailey, obviously."

"Is there nothing I can do?"

"I made my decision before coming here. I bought you a new identity. I have documents and a Swiss account for you." He reached into the box and showed me a leather handbag. "You can fly the plane. You have all the knowledge you need inside your head."

He was right, of course. I knew that. I had already been planning my escape. "Are you coming with me?" I said.

"They can't know I'm helping you. It's why I brought the gun, though I told them it was just to make you more suspicious, within the experiment," he said. "Use it to get away. I have to go back. I need to destroy everything."

I took his hand. "Alex. I modified my program. I'm Kailey again now. And Rose. Our thoughts are intermingling."

He stared at me for a long moment. "Are you certain Kailey wants this?" he said at last.

I nodded. "Neither of us could go back to the way we were. We're Aya now. A blend of our former selves."

"Are you happy, Aya?" He touched my cheek and peered into my eyes like he was trying to see each of us inside my head.

"Happy... but worried for the future."

"Do you know why I picked Kailey?" Alex's tone was gentle. "I read about the guard who raped her. I studied her case... I believed she was innocent. What I said before was for the cameras. I couldn't let them know I wanted to help her go free."

My heart was too full for me to speak. He gathered me in his arms, laid me down on the tarp, and lowered himself over me. I lost myself in the exquisite sensation of his hands and lips touching me. Under the half-light of the moon, he made tender love to me.

When we lay together afterwards, his whispered words swept over me. "We'll find each other again."

I grew tired as the plane neared the Philippines. Along with piloting, I had been "writing" Kailey's story in my memory to show Alex someday. I wasn't certain how much he really knew about her, other than what he'd surmised. I wanted him to fully understand who she was, and what her journey had been.

Soon I would land and show my papers. In the documents, I was "Susan Jones"—a name so generic it would be hard to trace. Alex had given me money for bribes as well. I fervently hoped there would be no problems. With freedom so close, it would be hard if it were taken away again.

Many uncertainties remained. The headaches returned from time to time. In the end, it might not be possible for Kailey's brain to bear the burden of another consciousness.

And I worried about Alex. The government operatives running his company sounded ruthless. What if they pressed criminal charges against him when he tried to destroy all his work? Or far worse, they might kill him. I would not be able to forgive myself if the last time I saw him turned out to be when I locked him in the latrine.

But life was full of fear and uncertainty. I'd been on the giving and receiving end of both. I didn't like either side of it, but I would deal with it if I had to.

With Alex the night before, and now in the plane gazing out at endless blue sea and sky, I succumbed to the giddy urge to hum a few of the tunes stored in my seemingly infinite memory. An overwhelming sense of lightness filled me. So much that I considered aiming the plane downwards and diving straight into the water, bringing an end to my life at the moment of my greatest joy.

I chose not to do it. Difficult times and more suffering might lie ahead, but the thought didn't frighten me anymore.

THE END
Read on for a preview of **LAST GIRL STANDING.**

LAST GIRL STANDING Preview

THE LOS PATOS Water Company is determined to poison us. Mom's words, not mine. She'd been saying it for so long, I still hesitated to drink the tap water. Even though no one in town had ever died of it, so far as I knew.

Feeling rebellious, I bent my head, ready to slurp from the faucet, when I glimpsed Mom's narrowed eyes watching me in the mirror. I changed my mind; it wasn't worth a shouting match. Instead, I splashed the water on my face as if I'd meant to do that all along. She continued down the hall, rebellion squelched before it began.

Dashing back to my room because I was running late as usual, I kicked aside the clothes on the floor to find my school books. I shoved them into my backpack, grabbed my cell, and raced to the kitchen. There I gulped a glass of filtered river water while Mom spread her homemade organic strawberry preserves on top of a slice of her homemade organic fifty-grain bread. Okay, maybe it wasn't fifty, but I lost count after ten.

She handed the toast to me. It tasted delicious, though sometimes I longed for a shiny sugary Pop-Tart, decorated with sprinkles the color of nothing you would ever find in nature, like my friend Giselle got to eat on a daily basis.

Mom twirled in front of me, modeling her outfit as she sometimes did when it was something new. "Do you like it, Sierra?"

I hadn't noticed the knitted whatever-it-was until now, because I was used to her looking pretty strange. At first, I thought she was wearing a blanket, but on closer inspection, it was a sort of fuzzy, purple/pink cape with armholes. "Um, nice," I managed to say, despite thinking it would take an apocalypse to get me to wear anything like it.

"I'm bringing it to Jane's Originals to see if they'll carry it."

"Good luck with that." I tried not to sound sarcastic as I shoved down the last bite of my toast.

She gripped my arm as I started to move past her. "Don't forget the water."

Of course I had forgotten the water. I usually hauled up a couple of buckets at the end of the day, but Mom had let me stay out past dinner the night before, on condition that I do my water shift before school.

"I'm late," I said.

But she just gave me the look that meant *you do this now, or there'll be trouble later.* She didn't care if I missed half of calculus, my first period class. Mom did not understand the value of any math beyond basic arithmetic. If my first class had been *How to Use a Spinning Wheel*, she would've prodded me out of bed an hour ago to be certain I didn't miss a second of that essential instruction.

I've known for some time that our family's not normal. It's just Mom and me and the hens and our goat, Brisa. Mom's an organic farmer and certifiable kook who would've fit in much better in the seventeenth century, before any modern conveniences were invented. According to her, we should all just grow our own food, find our own water, make our own clothes, build our own houses, and mind our own business. Well, maybe she would be willing to barter for some of those things she couldn't do herself.

Given her way of thinking, it was understandable she didn't trust water coming out of a tap. She posted this quote from Ian E. Stephens right next to our filter, to serve as a constant reminder of why we had to kill ourselves schlepping water from the river. The quote said, "Repeated doses of infinitesimal amounts of fluoride will in time reduce an individual's power to resist domination by slowly poisoning and narcotizing a certain area of the brain and will thus make him submissive to the will of those who wish to govern him." In other words, my mother believed water treated with fluoride could brainwash people.

We also had a rainwater collector behind the house, but so far we were having a dry winter and it hadn't rained in three weeks. Which was why I flung my backpack down on the chair, grabbed the clean water bucket, and rushed out the back door headed to the river.

The leaves were slippery due to being so dry, and as I hurried down the path, I suddenly found my feet shooting out from under me. *Crap.* I landed hard on my butt. I wasn't hurt, except for my self-esteem, but when I got up and tried to brush off the back of my pants, I realized I'd have to change them. *Great day to wear white.*

First I needed to get the water, because knowing me I was probably in for another fall before I made it back. In general, I was a klutz, and once or twice I'd even accidentally dunked myself in the river. Luckily the water didn't flow too hard in this section, and I was a good swimmer. But I wasn't taking any more chances today. I slowed as I reached the river bank.

The acacia tree across the water was in full display, its yellow flowers fluorescent in the dappled shade. I couldn't help but pause for a moment longer to take in the natural beauty of where we lived. The sound of the rushing river, the scent of the acacia blooms, the reflection of leaves in the silvery water where it pooled by the opposite shore... you'd have to be made of stone not to be moved by all this.

But calculus waited for no one, not even me with the best grade in the class so far. I swung the bucket into the water.

I saw it then. Ten yards upstream, a beige cloth or bag or something, caught on a short branch sticking out from one of the trees at the edge of the water. I was tempted to ignore it, but Mom had trained me too well about keeping the river clean. Especially if it might be plastic, I needed to fish it out. I put down my bucket and found a long stick—there was no shortage of them. Then I made my way along the river's edge till I was parallel with the floating thing.

A powerful stench, like a cross between a soiled diaper and rotting meat, clogged my nostrils and made me gag. I held my breath and spat, figuring the wind must've shifted and delivered the foul odor from somewhere across the river.

It was one more reason to hurry up and get out of there. I reached my stick over and snagged it on what definitely looked like clothing now, giving it a pull. The object rolled over, helped by the flowing water.

Something white and bloated and disgusting rose to the surface. Two eyes bulged and a tongue stuck out from what I realized must be the grotesque remains of a face.

My mouth dropped open and my breath caught in my throat. I tingled all over with pinpricks of dread. Then a shrill sound pierced my ears and I realized it was me screaming.

Please visit marjorykaptanoglu.com for purchase options.

Acknowledgments

Many thanks to The Book Reality Experience for their publishing expertise and assistance.

Much love and gratitude for the help and encouragement of these dear family, friends, and fellow authors:

Harriet S. Benedict, Giuliano Carlini, Vicki Cox, Sheri Davenport, Margaret Goldstein, Dan Goldstein, Evelyn Hail, Kay Liscomb, Ricki McGlashan, Cathy Murphy, Susan Rendina, Aimee Rosewood, Anu Roy, Karla Sheridan, Kurt Sutter, Cathy Thrush, Linda Wexler.

Mountains of love to my husband Sinan and sons Tanner, Alan, and Derek, without whom I couldn't manage any of this.

About the Author

Marjory Kaptanoglu is a novelist, screenwriter, and former Apple Computer software engineer. There was a time when she traveled a lot, but these days it's mostly in her head. She loves all fiction but tends to write in the sci-fi/fantasy genre. When not writing, she hangs out with family and friends, human and non-human.

Please write a review if you enjoyed this book. Reviews are incredibly important in helping newer authors build an audience. As my audience grows, I can spend less time on marketing, and more on writing new books.

Sign up at marjorykaptanoglu.com if you wish to be informed of new releases and upcoming sales.

Thank you for reading *Invader*!